Tulsa Tempest
The Tulsa Series #1
Norma Jean Lutz

Table of Contents

Publisher's Cataloging-In-Publication Data

Names: Lutz, Norma Jean, author.

Title: Tulsa tempest / Norma Jean Lutz.

Description: Owasso, OK : NUWSLink, Inc., [2017] | Series: The Tulsa series ; #1 | Originally published: Barbour Publishing, 1993.

Identifiers: ISBN 9780990803799 | ISBN 0990803791 | ISBN 9780985957148 (ebook)

Subjects: LCSH: Governesses—Oklahoma—Tulsa—History—20th century—Fiction. | African American household employees—Oklahoma—Tulsa—History—20th century—Fiction. | Teachers—Oklahoma—Tulsa—History—20th century—Fiction. | Interracial friendship—Oklahoma—Tulsa—History—20th century—Fiction. | Racism—Oklahoma—Tulsa—History—20th century—Fiction. | Tulsa (Okla.)—Race relations—History—20th century—Fiction. | LCGFT: Romance fiction. | Historical fiction.

Classification: LCC PS3562.U857 T85 2017 (print) | LCC PS3562.U857 (ebook) | DDC 813/.54—dc23

ISBN: 0-9908037-9-1

ISBN: 978-0-9908037-9-9

Tulsa Tempest originally published by Barbour Publishing, 1993

Note from The Author
Regarding the Tulsa Series

The 4-title Tulsa series has had a long and interesting journey. In the late 1990s, I had just completed the last of four contemporary romance novels for Barbour Publishing's *Heartsong* line. At that time, I was approached by my editor at Barbour to submit ideas to him for historical fiction.

Because I've lived in the Tulsa area for most of my adult life, I knew a little bit about the infamous Tulsa Race Riot of 1921. But honestly, at that time, no one talked much about it. (That later changed as survivors began to speak up.) I knew that that event would serve as the backdrop for my historical, Christian, Tulsa series.

The very same day that my editor asked me for historical fiction ideas, I sat down and wrote out thumbnail sketches for all four titles. He liked the ideas and offered a 4-book contract.

All four, then, were originally published through Barbour's *Heartsong* line where they enjoyed immense popularity. (I still have file folders full of fan letters.)

Later, when the idea of eBooks was in its infancy, an independent group offered to publish my series digitally. As often happens in the publishing industry, the whole thing fell apart due to 1) being ahead of the curve regarding digitally-produced books, and 2) poor business management.

And, yes, yet another group purporting to be an independent publisher, also had their hands in the pie. That too fell apart.

Discouraging to say the least.

The Tulsa Series languished until I recently resurrected them and placed them on Amazon's Kindle. Even with that, little was done to promote the titles.

But this is a new day!

Presently, the four titles are decked out in delightful new covers, plus all will now be available in both print *and* digitally.

I trust as a reader, you will enjoy these stories as much as I enjoyed researching and writing them.

You can connect with me here:

normajean@beanovelist.com

http://www.beanovelist.com/

https://www.facebook.com/BeANovelist/

http://normajeanlutz.com/

http://www.cleanteenreads.net/

https://www.facebook.com/CleanTeenReadsNet/

Chapter 1

Tessa was upset at Papa for ruining Christmas. Christmas should be a time for joy, not despair. Tessa's scuffed tan valise sat by the door waiting, her black cloth coat slung carelessly across it. The new red and blue muffler Mama had knitted for her for Christmas added a small bit of cheer.

"When are you coming back again, Tessie?" Vega wanted to know. Tessa felt her four-year-old sister tugging at her skirt as she tried to move about the cramped kitchen of their small house. Vega clutched the cloth doll Tessa had sewn for her as a Christmas gift. Christmas was two days ago, and Vega had not let loose of the doll since the moment she opened the package.

"She will be back when she can, Vega," Mama told her. "Just like always. As long as the roads stay open and Pastor Stedman can get through. Now scoot."

Tessa watched as little Vega stepped away long enough to have obeyed, then came back underfoot.

"Come over and color with me," eight-year-old Siegrid called out from the other side of the room. She was lying near the wood-burning stove to stay warm. She held up one of the bright crayons that Tessa brought from Independence School where she taught. Neither girl cared that they were broken.

Vega shook her head making the halo of blonde curls shake. Her clear blue eyes were wide. "I don't want to color. I want Tessie."

Tessa was trying to help Mama as much as she could before the rumble of Pastor Stedman's Model A sounded the warning that she must go. She folded the soft bread dough over and over again, while

Mama chopped the vegetables for the stew. Papa had shot a rabbit, and cleaned and dressed it. That would be their supper after Tessa left.

She traveled home from the Glenn Pool every weekend, but this time, since it was Christmas holiday, she was home longer. Perhaps that was why Vega now clung to her.

Looking down at Vega, she suddenly realized her little sister was troubled. Little ones could sense so much. Perhaps Vega had heard Tessa arguing with Papa last evening. Even if she didn't hear from the loft, Tessa believed her little spirit sensed something wasn't right.

Tessa lifted the fat mound of dough into the oiled crockery bowl, wiped her hands on the tea towel and sat down on one of the spindle chairs beside the kitchen table. Immediately Vega was on her lap. Tessa buried her nose in the little girl's silky curls. "When will you stay with us forever and ever, Tessie?"

Tessa looked over at Mama just in time to see her mother's gentle face cloud over with concern.

"You know I can't stay forever, Vega. I have to teach the children at the school at the Glenn Pool."

"But I want you to stay forever."

At that Siegrid dropped her crayon and came over to the chair and quietly stood behind Tessa. "At least until New Year's Eve," she added to Vega's plea.

Siegrid ran her finger around the crown of braids on top of Tessa's head. The braids loosened as Siegrid tugged at a hairpin. Siegrid gave a little giggle.

Tessa's hand flew up to the braid. "No, no, Siegrid. We can't play now. I've got to be ready."

She firmed the hairpin back in place.

"Last year you stayed until New Year's Eve," Siegrid persisted.

"Much warmer it was last holiday," Mama said. With her Swedish accent, Mama's w's all sounded like v's; but Tessa had been training herself and her sisters to pronounce their w's correctly.

"Hear that wind out there?" Tessa yanked one of Siegrid's long golden braids. "A storm may be coming. If it sleets or snows Pastor can't get through."

"Goody," Vega mimicked. "Pastor can't get through."

Tessa laughed and gave Vega a squeeze. Then she reached up and pulled Siegrid around where she could give her a hug. "Now girls, I need your help when I bring in another load of wood. Stand by the door and watch, and open quickly when I shout."

"Ve vill," Vega said as she hopped down.

"Wa, wa, will," Tessa corrected. She reached up to pull Mama's heavy woolen cloak down from the hook at the front door.

"Tessa," Mama chided with a shake of her head. "There's no need. I can do it."

"And you will do it—plenty times before winter is out."

"Wa, wa, will," Vega chanted as she danced about with her dolly as a partner.

"If Berg were still with us..." Siegrid said.

"No if's, little sister. Berg is warm and happy in heaven, and he doesn't have to cut or carry any wood." She fastened the hood of the cloak securely under her chin. "Now mind you, open as soon as I shout."

She heard the girls giggling as they slammed the door behind her. Cold wind hit her face like a thousand tiny needles. She hurried down the stoop and across the barren yard to the woodpile. She, too, missed Berg. It was because of him she made the decision to teach. When pneumonia took his life winter before last, she was determined she must earn money to help Mama and the girls. Even at fourteen, Berg was straight and strong as a towering oak. No one would have thought such a healthy boy would be felled by an illness.

Kneeling down, she carefully selected the biggest logs she could possibly carry. She balanced them on one arm and piled them up. Using her other arm to cradle them, she slowly pushed up to her feet again.

The weight pulled at her back. She tottered a moment, but caught her balance.

At least she needn't worry about stumbling over Old Blue, Papa's hound. He was probably sitting proudly in the buckboard wherever Papa was—whatever he was doing. She kicked the cloak out of the way before stepping up on the stoop so as not to trip.

"Open," she shouted. The door flew open without a moment's hesitation. She staggered to the heating stove where the girls dutifully unloaded her arms. Together they made a neat stack that would last through the night.

As she hung Mama's heavy cloak back in its place, she heard the unmistakable sound of the Model T. She saw both girls freeze.

Mama hurriedly pulled the warm bricks from the oven. Wrapped in old rags, the bricks would keep Tessa's feet warm at least half the way to the Pastor's house.

Tessa wound the warm woolen muffler around her head and neck before pulling on her coat. By the time she had pulled on her knitted mittens, she heard Pastor's strong knock on the door.

"Ho, ho," he called out with laughter ringing in his voice. Pastor Stedman was always laughing. "Guess who?"

As she opened it, the noise of the rattling old car filled the house. A hearty gust of north wind ushered the Pastor in. His huge frame made the house seem even smaller. The aroma of gasoline permeated his coat and hat. He pulled the door shut behind him. He politely removed the hat to reveal a shock of snow white hair.

"Welcome Pastor Stedman," Mama said as she stepped from the kitchen to the doorway to shake his hand. "I have *pepparkakors* for you to take back for you and Edith to enjoy."

Pastor patted his front and his smile beamed beneath the white fluffy mustache. "Still trying to fatten me up, eh Gerda Jurgen? Vell, it's vorking," he said mocking her Swedish pronunciations.

Mama gave him a kind smile and the girls giggled.

"And vat are you two giggling about?" Pastor's hand dug deep into his coat pocket. "I say, Siegrid, have you grown two inches since I was here last?"

Siegrid shook her head and blushed.

"She's almost as tall as Tessa," Vega offered.

"That's not saying much," Pastor said, his grin now aimed right at Tessa. "To be as big as a peanut."

The girls giggled again, but Tessa didn't mind. She never minded Pastor's teasing. It was always in love. Unlike Papa's teasing.

Pastor continued to fish about in his pocket as the girls watched closely. "Would you look here," he said acting surprised. "How do you suppose these came to be in the pocket of this coat?" His wide fist was thrust out. The girls ventured closer.

He opened his hand to offer them each a piece of peppermint stick. Vega jumped forward to take the candy; Siegrid moved more cautiously.

"What do you tell Pastor?" Mama encouraged. She was still scurrying about getting everything ready for Tessa to take.

"Tank you, Pastor Stedman," Siegrid said softly, and an echo came from Vega. They looked at Mama for permission to eat them now. Mama nodded.

"Wish I could stay and visit, Gerda, but those clouds look mighty threatening. And Tin Lizzie is leaping to get back home."

"Go," Mama said. "I help carry." She pulled her cloak down from the hook and spread it around her. "Siegrid, help with the door again. Close it tightly until I come back in."

Pastor grabbed the valise, and the basket of food Mama had prepared. Mama took the warmed bricks. Tessa kissed her sisters and then grabbed up the box of her belongings, which was tied with twine. Last night Mama had urged her to take a few more of her possessions back to the parsonage. Especially the books.

"Our house is so little," Mama told her. "You may as well help us out by taking these with you."

Strange, Tessa thought. Everything was so strange this time. The wind coming across the fields was almost too cold to allow words of good-by to Mama. The wind sucked the very air from her lungs.

Tessa settled into the front seat as Mama positioned the warm bricks beneath her feet. Pastor Stedman brought out the heavy lap robe and the two of them tucked her in as though she were a child getting ready for bed.

Before closing the door, Mama took Tessa's face in her hands and whispered. "It is sorry Papa is not here."

Tessa nodded but found no words to answer. It was all right with her that he was not there. But she knew what Mama meant. Mama was really saying she wished Papa were more of a papa, not just that moment, but all the time.

Tessa felt suspended between two worlds. The pull forward to the kindness and gentleness of the Stedman home near the Glenn Pool. The pull back to the love of her mother and sisters, and her need to help them. Each time, the pulling ripped at her insides until she wasn't sure where she truly belonged. "I love you Mama," she said.

"You are my Tiny Delight, Tessa. God bless you." She released Tessa and closed the door and scurried back into the house.

As the pastor settled in and the old car moved away, Tessa wiped steam off the window and saw Siegrid and Vega with their faces pressed again the window watching her go. Tessa knew they were crying. She felt a pang of remorse because she didn't share that same deep sadness with them.

The car moved slowly through the rolling hills, which were covered by stands of scrub oak and blackjack with a few taller cottonwoods among them, now all barren in the winter chill. Nothing was as colorless as Oklahoma in the winter. Mama always said that at least in Sweden there was pretty snow all winter. Tessa watched as the endless miles of brown countryside moved by her window. An occasional farmhouse, or a line of trees along a creek bank, broke the monotony. The heavy gray clouds caused the horizon to fade into a colorless nothing.

The aroma of Mama's sweet *lussikatter*, and *pepparkakors* mixed in with the harsh smell of gasoline and made Tessa's stomach do strange things. The special buns and cookies were part of Mama's tradition to celebrate St. Lucia's Day, and she had carefully saved back enough to share with Pastor and Edith.

When Tessa was small, the story of the young St. Lucia kept her in awe. But now that she was older, now that Pastor Stedman and Edith had made Jesus so real to her, Mama's traditions from the Old Country had lost their effect on her.

Pastor Stedman hummed hymns deep in his throat as he wrestled with the steering wheel of the old car. Tessa knew before they traveled very far, he would begin singing. This was just the warm-up time.

Tessa wished her family had a car, even if it were an old Model T like this one. Mama could learn to drive and do more things for herself. A telephone would be nice, too.

By the time the bricks cooled, Tessa's body heat beneath the weight of the lap robe had warmed her some. Even though the car broke the wind better than when they all piled into Papa's wagon, it was still a biting cold. Periodically she rubbed her hands together or rubbed her cold nose with the warm mitten.

Soon Pastor Stedman was singing, beginning with mild renditions of "Yield Not to Temptation," and "The Lily of the Valley." By the time they reached the parsonage, he would be into gusty songs like "Awakening Chorus." But midway into "Since Jesus Came Into My Heart" he stopped.

He glanced over at her—even though he could scarcely afford to take his eyes from the deep, frozen ruts in the road. "Say Little One, why so quiet? My singing sounds so much better when your singing comes along side to soften it."

She smiled. "Don't stop," she told him. "It makes me feel better inside."

"You need to feel better?" The question hung in the cold air. Tessa didn't quite know how to answer, so she remained quiet.

Pastor was kind and changed the subject. "The school board met the other day," he told her, "and voted to renew your contract for the nineteen twenty-one, twenty-two school year." He gave a hearty laugh. "When they first laid eyes on you almost a year and half ago, they had a few misgivings. Tiny thing that you are, and so young. But now they're proud as banty roosters—even old Hargis—acting like it was all their idea."

Mr. Hargis owned the mercantile store near the Glenn Pool where the main cluster of oilfield workers lived. He had been the most vocal. Mr. Hargis said that at age sixteen, Tessa would never be able to handle the rowdy children of the oil field roughnecks and roustabouts. The children had such unsettled lives moving about from one oilfield to the next—wherever there was work. But she proved she could do the work. Now they wanted her to stay. And now she could no longer stay.

"I figured you'd be spouting 'I told you so's' when you heard. A third year they want you, Little One."

She didn't know what to say. Finally, when she could stand the silence no more, she said softly, "I can't come back next fall, Pastor. I'm sorry."

But Pastor's hearing wasn't all that good, and the noise of the infernal engine was horrid. He cupped his ear and leaned in her direction. "What's that, Little One?"

So she had to say it again. Louder. And it hurt worse to say it the second time. "I can't come back."

"Can't come back? Now why on earth can't you?"

She chose her words carefully. "Papa has other plans for me. Come May, I'm to marry Hod Latham."

At that, Tessa feared the pastor was headed clean off the road. "Hod Latham? You can't mean it. Lord forgive me, but that man has the worst reputation in the county. Everybody knows he's one of the most rambunctious bootleggers around, and mean as a hornet."

"And so is Papa."

Chapter 2

Pastor Stedman never got around to singing "Awakening Chorus." By the time they turned in the long drive to the Stedman house, he was fairly fuming. Tessa couldn't remember ever seeing Pastor so upset. She had assumed she would tell him about Hod, and that would be that. But that wasn't that.

Dusk was settling in around them and soft lights glowed their welcome in the downstairs windows of the parsonage. She saw Edith's form move past the bay windows in the parlor. Tessa knew she was waiting for their arrival. The front door flung open almost before the car stopped. Edith, wrapped in her long fringed shawl, was there helping Tessa with her things.

"Welcome home dear," she said as they made their way up the walk to the door. "I've missed you."

Tessa had missed Edith too. She was almost afraid to admit how much.

After they unloaded, Pastor drove the Model T behind the house and into the shed. Tessa could hear him call from the kitchen as he came in the back door. "I'm ready for my cup of hot cocoa, Edith. Come on in here, we need to talk."

Edith sent a glance to Tessa. "Is something wrong?" When Tessa had no answer, Edith reached out to gently take her coat and muffler. "Let me hang these up for you. Ah, a lovely muffler. From Mama for Christmas?"

Tessa nodded. "And the mittens."

"Such a blessing to have so much love wrapped around you."

Tessa hadn't thought of it quite like that, but it was true. She was wrapped securely in Mama's love.

When they were seated at the kitchen table warming themselves with the mugs of hot cocoa, Pastor looked at Edith. "Mrs. Stedman," he declared, "our little friend here is facing a colossal problem."

Edith reached out and covered Tessa's hand. "Problem? My goodness, you're too young to have big problems."

"And this one is a whole lot bigger than she can handle alone," Pastor continued. "Her father has promised her hand in marriage to Hod Latham."

"Hod Latham?" Edith's grip tightened. "But that's impossible. No father would..." She stopped. "I'm so sorry my dear."

Tessa nodded. Of course, no father should do such a thing. But her father had. She assumed it was some business deal gone sour and now Papa somehow owed Hod, and this was how he planned to make it good. No matter. Knowing the details wouldn't change things.

"Prohibition is made to order for scoundrels such as Latham and his ilk," Edith said. "That amendment seems to have produced more problems than it solved."

"Tessa," Pastor said in a tone graver than she'd ever heard him use, even behind the pulpit, "I think we need to get you out of here."

Edith patted her hand. "He's right Tessa. We'll have to get you out of the county as quickly as possible. Before your Papa even realizes you're gone."

"Go away? But where?"

Pastor drained the last of his cocoa and set the mug down with great emphasis. "I have no idea just now, Little One, but God knows. We'll trust Him to show us. Now let's bring Him in on the scene." He stretched his big hand across the table to Tessa. They held hands and bowed their heads as Pastor prayed in his booming voice so that Tessa was sure those in the next homestead could hear. He quoted a bevy of scriptures having to do with guidance and deliverance. Tessa had never met anyone so full of scripture as Pastor Stedman.

When the prayer was finished, he was smiling. "There now," he said as though it were settled. "You can sleep easy tonight. Nobody's going to make you marry a man like Hod Latham. To marry means to become one, and how can darkness be joined to light?"

"I'll fix your lamp, Tessa," Edith said. "I know you're tired."

Tessa was grateful for Edith's sensitivity. Even though it was barely eight, even though she had nothing for which to rise early the next morning, she was ready to crawl into bed. When she was in this house of love, her burden for Mama and the girls was lessened. Not completely erased, but eased some.

"We're having the Church Sing here tomorrow night," Edith said. "Will you feel up to it? There'll be about twenty."

Tessa managed a weak smile. "I'll be fit as a fiddle in the morning. You'll need a hand with the baking."

As she turned to go, pastor put up his hand to make one closing remark. "It's not that we're forcing you to go anywhere. In the end it will be your decision to make."

She nodded and opened the door to the stairwell. Pastor had already taken her things to her room which was upstairs at the end of the hall. There were four upstairs bedrooms which previously belonged to the four Stedman sons, all of whom were married and gone. Edith often told Tessa that she was the daughter Edith had always longed for.

The coal oil lamp created dancing shadows in the friendly room which served as her home away from home. She sat down on the edge of her bed and pulled hairpins from the long braids atop her head. She felt so safe in this room. Could Pastor be serious about her leaving?

She had always been terrified of Hod, even when she was a little girl. Hod was built like a block of granite, with a thick neck and a barrel chest. Under his straw hat, his hair was scraggly and unkempt. His coloring was dark, and some said he was part Indian, but no one knew for sure. Most people stayed shy of Hod Latham—everyone, that is, except for Papa.

Hod was bow-legged from riding his old mule all around the country side. Tessa remembered how Berg used to mock Hod's funny walk, and they would laugh till their sides ached. If Berg were still alive, he wouldn't be laughing now. And he'd never allow Papa to follow through with this terrible deal.

Tessa moved to the window. The thick low clouds were breaking apart and a slivered moon peeked through. Soft warm lights from the adjoining homestead shone through the scant stand of trees. Orange lights from the oil derricks of the Glenn Pool flickered in the distance. In warm weather, with the windows open, they could hear the pounding of the rigs, drilling deep to search out the black gold.

Pastor seemed confident that God would find a place for her to go, but she was praying God would create a way for her to stay. What would the children at the one-room school do without her? She'd worked so hard to bring them into a place where each one was excelling in at least one or two subjects.

The thought of leaving was almost as frightening as the thought of marrying Hod. She turned the wick down on the lamp and crawled under the comforter and sunk into the feather mattress. Her last thoughts before falling asleep were of Siegrid and Vega sleeping on the straw ticking in their drafty house, while she was snug and warm in luxury.

When she came down to breakfast the next morning, Pastor had newspapers spread across the kitchen table. He subscribed to at least three and read them thoroughly. "My Lord in heaven," she heard him mutter.

"What is it, Royce?" Edith asked from across the room.

"Another lynching of a black man." The pastor thumped at the table for emphasis. "And the *Tulsa World* seems to encourage the lawlessness. Why don't those Tulsa law enforcement officers put a stop to this?"

"Why don't they?" Tessa asked as she came in the kitchen.

Pastor pulled off his eyeglasses and looked up at her. "Good morning, Little One. You better?"

She nodded. "Much better. I hope I wasn't too vacant last evening." She turned to Edith who was tending the frying pork at the stove. "I'm afraid I didn't give you much of a healthy greeting."

"Pawsh. It was healthier than I would have given had I been burdened with the news you received."

The welcome morning sun pouring in through the kitchen windows, glistened on the linoleum-covered floor. Tessa fetched her apron from the hook by the gas stove, pulled it over her head and tied the sash. "Want me to start the eggs?"

Edith nodded.

"Why do they allow lynchings?" Tessa asked again. Pastor once told her that people turned out for a lynching as they would for a sideshow. She shuddered at the mere thought. How could anyone enjoy seeing another suffer?

"Hate and greed mostly. There's a lot of money up there in Tulsa. Maybe all that money is buying favors." He thumped at the paper again. "But for the newspapers to wink at it..." His voice trailed off as he rubbed his bushy mustache. "How it must grieve the heart of the Father God—men hating their fellow man." From the ice box, Tessa lifted out the bowl of eggs. Cracking four into a smaller bowl she beat them vigorously. The kitchen was quiet except for the sizzling of the pork, and the coffee pot perking.

"Say, Little One." Pastor's voice broke the silence. "Would you listen to this ad? I've been up since the wee hours praying about your situation regarding that no-count Hod Latham. Could this be God's answer?"

He hooked his wire-rimmed eye glasses around his ears, firmed them up on his nose, and read: "'Oil magnate family in Tulsa desires services of young female as nanny and tutor for two small children. Good salary and private quarters. Candidates inquire at the Patton mansion, Riverview area, 14th and Galveston. No cursing, smoking, or drinking.'" He paused and looked up from the paper. "What do you think? Sounds promising, would you agree?"

Tessa stopped beating the eggs. Tulsa? Tulsa was a long way off. She felt both pairs of eyes on her, but she wasn't sure what she was supposed to say. This was all so sudden. Everything in her life was so perfect. She loved her work at the Independence school, she loved her home here with the Stedmans. How could she just leave? What would the school board think? What would Mama think?

"That paper's a day old. Perhaps they've found a girl by now," Tessa offered. She poured the whipped eggs into the waiting cast-iron skillet and heard the pleasant sizzle. Usually the aromas of breakfast were tantalizing to her. But now her stomach was churning as it had last evening in the Model T.

"How about if I drive out to the oil field this morning and see if I can find someone who works for Patton Oil," Pastor suggested. "Those roustabouts know everything that goes on in Tulsa. If I snoop around a bit, perhaps I can learn something."

Edith lifted the pork onto the rose-patterned platter as Tessa filled the mugs with hot coffee. Tessa stretched to her full five foot to pull the plate of thick bread slices from the warming oven, then she scooped the scrambled eggs into a serving bowl.

Pastor cleared the newspapers from the table and stacked them on the sideboard. As he bowed his head to offer thanks, he again asked for guidance for Tessa.

"Pastor," she said as she forced herself to eat, "it doesn't seem exactly honest to run away. Is that Christian? I mean is that what God would want?"

"Of course not," his deep voice boomed out. "God doesn't want you to have to leave. That's not what He would want at all. But when there are people like Hod Latham in this world, we must act accordingly."

He cut his fried pork into precise pieces. "There's a passage in the book of Acts," he said, "where it tells about when the Apostle Paul began preaching with great zeal. He kindled such terrible hatred in the hearts of the locals, that his friends decided to sneak him out of town in a basket. Remember?"

He needn't ask. She'd heard the story countless times during the long winter evenings when Pastor and Edith read aloud from the Word.

"No Tessa, God doesn't want people to have to run, but sometimes there's no choice. But God's always there to guide and protect."

Edith reached over and gave Tessa's arm a gentle pat. "I believe the Lord will provide a basket of safety in which our Tessa may escape."

Chapter 3

The day dragged as Tessa found little things to keep her hands busy. The baking was done before they shared a light lunch. In the afternoon, she sat by the wood-burning stove and continued knitting the pair of stockings she'd begun before Christmas. Edith didn't force conversation. That was so like her to leave Tessa to her own thoughts.

It was almost four when they heard the Model T rumble up the drive. Tessa felt herself tense. Rather than hurrying to the door, Edith came and put her hand on Tessa's shoulder. "Shall we go see what Pastor's learned?"

Together they met him at the back door. The brief sunshine from the morning hours had been overtaken by heavy clouds. The air felt damp.

"Howdy," he called as he got out of the car.

"Aren't you going to drain the radiator and put it away?" Edith asked.

He pulled his hat off as he came through the door. "Mmm. Smells good in here. I'll not put the car away quite yet. I may have one more errand to run."

"Don't forget, guests will arrive at seven."

"I've not forgotten one thing, my dear. One step at a time. One step at a time." He turned to Tessa. "As far as I can learn, the job at the Patton's is still open."

He led her to a kitchen chair and had her sit down.

"Coffee?" Edith asked.

Pastor shook his head. "Later." He hadn't taken his coat off. "Tessa this must be your decision and yours alone. We can help you, but you must be agreeable to the plan. I can't force you to do something you

20

don't want to do." He smiled. "I don't think they stuffed the Apostle Paul into that basket, do you? At some point, he had to make the decision to crawl in."

"Do you have a plan?" Perhaps he was going to drive her up to Tulsa himself and see to it that she was taken care of.

He nodded and scooted his chair closer to hers. "There's a man from a company in Tulsa who delivers produce to Hargis every Wednesday. If you want to try to make a go of it in Tulsa, I'll go ask Hargis what the chances are of your getting a ride."

She was quiet as thoughts raced through her head. How could she ride with a man she'd never met?

But Pastor read her mind. "Hargis knows him well, and I've met him too. Mr. Dixson's a nice old guy. I'm sure he can be trusted. Otherwise I wouldn't have suggested it."

"You can pack a few things that you'll need, Tessa," Edith said, "and we can send the rest to you as soon as you're settled in somewhere."

Tessa caught the word "somewhere." She knew without asking that there was no guarantee she would get this particular job. But somehow they seemed sure she would be able to find something. And because they believed it, she found she could believe it too. After all, everyone said there were plenty of jobs in the "Magic City." She could even run an elevator if she had to. She knew how to work hard. Someone would hire her. Suddenly she was nodding. She'd show Hod Latham a thing or two. And Papa, too.

Pastor caught her shoulders and gave a squeeze. "That's my girl." He jumped to his feet. "I'm heading for Hargis's store, Edith. I'll be back in a short shake." He took out a pitcher of warm water to pour in the radiator before cranking the Model T one more time.

Later that evening, the parsonage was filled with cheery voices. "We must carry on as though nothing is amiss," Edith told her when the first guests began to arrive. Then she whispered softly, "You can do it."

But now Tessa wasn't sure. Tears were near the surface all evening. All of these community people had become dear friends. And suddenly she was leaving.

It was difficult to concentrate on the conversation that was being aimed at her. She was grateful when they finally gathered in the parlor around the pump organ and began to sing the hymns they all loved. She no longer had to talk.

At one point as they were singing, "Where He Leads Me, I Will Follow," she glanced up and saw Edith gazing at her. There were tears in her eyes. Tessa couldn't finish the song because of the growing lump in her throat.

WEDNESDAY MORNING DAWNED bleak and gray. Tessa had so hoped for bright sunshine.

"If we load you in that produce truck in front of Hargis Mercantile," Pastor said at the breakfast table, "there's no telling who might see and go right out and spout it to your Papa. We'll meet him at Lone Grove Crossroads north of town after he makes his delivery."

Tessa tried desperately to eat the hot oatmeal, but couldn't. Pastor finished his and shoved the bowl back. He went to the sideboard and opened the top drawer, pulling out an envelope. "I've put a little cash together as sort of a bonus for you for all your hard work at the school."

He handed her the envelope. She could feel it was fat with bills.

"If necessary you can go to the YWCA and stay for a night or two. It's at fifth and Cheyenne. I'll write it on the envelope." He took a stub of a pencil from his pocket. "The other is a letter of recommendation signed by me and Hargis."

"Thank you very much." Tessa felt a catch in her throat. "You've been more than kind to me. How can I ever repay you?"

"Just keep your eyes on Jesus," Pastor said.

Too soon, she and Pastor were crawling into the cold automobile. Edith told her to layer her woolen clothing. "The more you wear, the less you need to pack," came the sage advice.

Tessa hugged Edith and struggled to hold back the burning tears. Edith's gentle kiss brushed her cheek. "The Lord will watch over you to keep you in all your ways," she said. As they drove off, Tessa looked back at her standing in the cold air, waving.

When they arrived in town, Pastor motored down main street and there was the produce truck parked at Hargis's store. "Right on time," Pastor commented. As he drove north out of town, he said to her, "Set your mind on that tutoring job at the Patton's. I know you can do it, and you'll be a blessing to those children."

"Yes sir."

He left the Model T running and pulled out the Thermos and poured each of them a cup of steaming hot cocoa. Tessa drank hers quickly before it cooled off.

Just as Pastor was putting the Thermos away, they heard the rumble of the produce truck approaching. It came to a stop beside them. It was the Dawes Produce Company truck all right, but there was a young man at the wheel.

The young man opened the door on the driver's side and stood up on the running board. "You Pastor Stedman?" he called out.

"I am. And where is Mr. Dixson?"

"The old man is in bed with the grippe. I had to take his place today. I understand you got a rider to go to Tulsa."

Tessa felt a clutching at her heart. For a moment, she thought Pastor would change his mind and stop the whole thing. Perhaps next week Mr. Dixson would be here and she could ride with him. Pastor turned to her and said softly, "The Lord will watch over you. Are you ready?"

She nodded.

Pastor got out and lifted her valise and the carpet satchel into the back of the truck. There were bits and pieces of old lettuce and a couple of rotten apples scattered about. She hoped it wouldn't stain the satchel—a gift from Edith.

Pastor Stedman opened the door and helped Tessa up into the delivery truck. "And your name, young man?"

"Jack Hansley."

"Jack, do you have a lap robe for this young lady?"

"Heck fire, no." Jack quickly caught himself. "No sir," he corrected. "No need for no lap robe in this old thing. We never have no riders."

"Wait a moment, please." Pastor stepped back to the Model T to get their lap robe.

Jack was already fidgeting. "I gotta get back before this storm comes in," he shouted out at Pastor. But the older man took his time covering Tessa and tucking her in, ignoring her protests at taking their fine lap robe.

"God be with you, my dear. Call the Hargis Store if you need anything."

"I will. Good-bye." The truck was already chugging down the road before she could get the last word out. She patted her coat pocket where the envelope lay safe beneath the lap robe.

Chapter 4

Jack's voice droned on as he talked about nothing in particular. He seemed to like the sound of his own voice. His face was narrow and angular, his long nose reddened from the cold. He claimed to know all there was to know about how the produce trucks operated and claimed he could fix anything that went wrong. Tessa assumed that meant he was the mechanic who just happened to be chosen to fill in as a driver.

The truck was not as tightly enclosed as the Model T. Icy wind blew in freely around the flaps that hung down over the side windows. Tessa forced herself to keep wiggling her fingers and toes. But soon she couldn't tell whether or not her toes were even moving.

Tiny beads of sleet pinged against the windshield. Several times the young driver stopped the truck and attempted to scrape a spot clean with a board he kept down by his feet. The delays were agonizing. Dark would come early. She must quickly find out if she had a chance for the job at the Patton's and if not, then plan to go to the YWCA for the night.

The cold air seemed to be freezing her mind as well. It was difficult to plan rationally. By the time they passed the sign indicating the Tulsa city limits, her feet were quite numb.

"You ever been to Tulsa before?" Jack asked, turning the subject away from himself for the first time.

She nodded. "The summer of Nineteen-nineteen. When the soldiers came home and paraded down main street." In the foggy distance, the tall lighted buildings of downtown Tulsa came into view.

"Is that right? I was there, too. Somewhere in that giant crowd, we were both there." His voice held a note of amazement. "Just think of that."

Tessa couldn't think of that. She wasn't sure what he meant anyway. She was trying to plan just how she would talk to Mr. Patton. Her bottom hurt from bouncing around on the hard truck seat for so long.

"And now," Jack was continuing, "fate has brought us together again." He steered the truck over the Arkansas River bridge. "You sure got purty blue eyes. Anybody ever tell you how purty your eyes are?"

Mama and the girls told her that all the time, but she was sure that wasn't what Mr. Jack Hansley meant. She didn't answer. He turned north at the intersection of 21st and Main. Pastor had explained to her how neatly the Tulsa streets were laid out. Fourteenth street would not be far from 21st. But when Jack came to Fourteenth, he did not slow down or turn. Pastor had told him specifically where she was to be taken.

"The Patton mansion is on Fourteenth," she told him sharply. Now that they were on paved streets the ride was not so bumpy. He could turn and look at her. He gave a big smile which showed a broken tooth. "You don't know much about Tulsa," he said. "Fourteenth don't even go through to Galveston."

She didn't know whether to believe him or not. Fear, mingled with anger rose up inside her. "Then what street does go through?" she demanded.

"Now, now, not to worry. Old Jack knows Tulsa like the back of his hand. I'll get you there all safe and sound."

The truck continued to lumber up Main as Tessa watched the street signs go from Thirteenth all the way to Ninth. Panic squeezed in her throat. "Where are you going? Pastor showed me a map and this is the wrong way."

Suddenly, he careened the truck down an alley between tall buildings, stopped and put it in gear and gave her another grin. "I've did you a big favor bringing you all this way. And I think you owe me a little something." He slid over in the seat and put his arm across the seat in back of her, but she slunk back against the door.

"Pastor Stedman paid you for your trouble. You were told to take me to the Patton mansion." She attempted to use her school teacher tone.

"But the old man ain't here."

"Stay away from me."

"Just one little kiss ain't going to hurt nothing. Just one."

Now he was pressed up close beside her. She could smell his rancid breath. With all her strength, she lifted the heavy wool robe from her lap and slung it over his head, then reached to the floor and grabbed Jack's board. In spite of numb fingers, she swung it hard as she could up aside his head. She felt the jolt go all the way to her shoulder. He let out a terrible yowl.

"Stop that, you little witch. All I wanted was one measly kiss."

As he struggled to get out of the blanket, she swung one more time for good measure and he yelped again. Opening the door, she jumped down, unsure if her frozen feet would hold her. Willing her legs to walk, she grabbed her two bags from the back, and ran down the alley.

"Come back here, you little witch!" he called after her.

As she reached Main Street, she heard the motor of the truck sputter, then die. Served him right. In this cold, he'd probably never get it started. She heard him spewing out a string of curse words as he tried to crank it up again.

The signs at the corner said Ninth and Main. She looked down Main Street where each streetlight shone softly in the evening dusk. Cheery Christmas decorations glittered in store windows, but she had no time to admire them. She headed back toward Tenth. Jack had said Fourteenth didn't go through, but she knew the mansion overlooked the river. If she walked back to the river, then she could find it. A roustabout at the oil field told Pastor the mansion was so big a blind man couldn't miss it.

As she walked, the feeling slowly came back into her feet, but it was sharp pain. Each toe screamed in protest. After she'd gone a couple of blocks, she stopped and put her woolen muffler up over her head. Tiny flecks of sleet stung her cheeks. She picked up the bags and straightened herself. She'd been cold before. She could make it.

The best thing to do, she reasoned, was to get back to the bridge at 21st then follow the road by the river until she saw the mansion. She doubted that Jack would follow her.

The streets were growing slick, forcing her to choose her steps with great care. She turned north at the Riverside Drive. Now she felt she was on the right track.

Darkness settled down around her with a kind of finality. Gleaming across the river were the lights from the refineries. Some had orange flames shooting from the tops. Their reflections shimmered on top the black water. To her right the glow of city lights reflecting off low-hanging clouds, created a lovely pink effect.

The heavy bags pulled at her arms, and she was forced to periodically set them down and rest. Each time it was more difficult to pick them up.

Presently, she heard a rumbling coming from behind her. Surely that couldn't be Jack. A shiver ran through her. In this big city, who knew what might happen? Faint lights from behind grew steadily brighter. She moved off the side of the road.

It was a red roadster which pulled to a stop beside her, but she chose to keep walking. "Hey," a man's voice called through the cranked-down window. "Little girl, where are you going?" She kept walking, but the car crept forward to where she was. "Are you running away from home? May I help?"

That's probably exactly what she looked like—a little girl running away from home. She looked over to see a young man who quickly doffed his hat, to reveal a full head of dark brown hair. His smile was friendly.

"There are no hotels out this way," he said. "No boarding houses either. And the YWCA is a very long way from here. I'd be pleased to give you a ride."

"No thank you," she said. What she didn't need was another wrestling match. She trudged forward.

"Suit yourself." He rolled up the window and drove on.

The road grew into a slight incline, and Tessa wondered if she could make it. She put the bags down and massaged her arms, then picked them up again. Presently two dim headlights could be seen ahead coming at her from the opposite direction. Once more she stepped off to the side.

The same red roadster pulled to a stop. Now the driver's side was next to her. He rolled down the window. "Little girl," he said, "I don't know why you decided to run away. Lots of young girls come to Tulsa thinking they can get work, but it's not that easy. Are you lost? If you keep going this way, you're going to freeze to death. There's nothing out this way."

"Please mind your own business. I know where I'm going. I'll thank you to leave me alone." She looked at him again. Now she could see his smiling brown eyes. "And I'm *not* a little girl," she added, and kept walking.

"One couldn't tell by looking. I bet you're not a day over thirteen."

She stopped short. "I happen to be nineteen. I'm an adult, I know where I'm going, and I know what I'm doing. Now please get out of here and stop pestering me."

A ride would be wonderful, but she was no dummy. Just because she was from out in the country, didn't mean she could be duped twice in one day.

Gears ground as he put the roadster in reverse. The car was beside her once again. "I can't just leave you out here all alone."

"Of course you can," she said firmly, stepping up her pace. The nerve of some people.

Resignation sounded in his voice as he said, "Have it your way, little girl. Don't say old Gaven MacIntyre didn't try. See you around."

Once the car was gone, the darkness seemed darker than ever, and it was only about seven o'clock. Later, she almost wished she'd accepted the ride. She had thought there would be side streets intersecting with Riverside Drive, but there were none for quite a way.

Just when she thought she couldn't take another step, she saw a signpost ahead, and an intersecting road. She hurried toward it. It was Galveston. And there to her right, high atop the hill, was the mansion. In spite of the cold, she stopped and stared. It was like a picture from a fairy tale.

The massive rock and brick edifice stretched out across the top of the hill. Sharply pointed gables pointed toward the night sky, and every window in the house was alive with yellow light. At one end, a broad covered portico, supported by fat white columns, provided a place where the motor cars could stop and passengers could step out protected from the weather.

Tessa turned up Galveston. Her shoulders and back ached with a deep pain. The property was surrounded by an ornate wrought iron fence protruding upward from a brick and stone base.

A wide gate spanned the driveway at the front. Tessa made her way to the top of the hill, where she unlatched a small gate in the fence and made her way down the brick driveway to the covered portico. A number of expensive automobiles were parked in the area behind the house.

The wide portico provided relief from the biting wind and stinging sleet. She resisted the temptation to rest, but rather followed the sidewalk from the side portico around to the front. The entry porch, nearly as wide as the portico, was supported by the same type of white stately columns. She hurried up the wide stone steps.

There through the tall front windows, she could see a magnificent Christmas tree in the front room decorated with electrical lights. She'd heard of electric decorations on Christmas trees, now she would see it for herself. Tessa marveled that one family lived in such a huge house. She wished Vega and Siegrid could see it with her.

There were sounds of happy voices and soft music coming from inside. Setting her bags down by her side, she pulled the bell cord. Suddenly the door was opened by the tallest black man she'd ever seen. She jumped back and gasped. The man looked down at her, his eyes wide with surprise and disbelief. He was impeccably dressed in a spiffy dark suit.

"Would you look at that," he said, looking down at her and shaking his head. Then he looked out beyond her as though to search where she'd come from. "Why little missy, it's mighty cold to be out strolling around on a nasty night like this. What you doing out here all alone?"

Tessa knew she must look a fright. How she wished she could have made herself more presentable. "I'm Miss Tessa Jurgen. I've come to interview for the position of nanny and tutor for the Patton children. It was advertised in the *Tulsa World.*"

"Why, yes little missy it was, but it's an opening for an experienced school marm." As he spoke, a yapping white terrier appeared behind him. Tessa had never seen such a cute little dog—much prettier than Papa's coon hounds. "Hush now, Kipsee," the black man ordered the dog. But the yapping dog ignored him.

"I *am* experienced," she said. "Please show this letter to Mr. Patton." She reached in her pocket for the letter of recommendation. But the pocket was empty. She felt the other pocket; it was empty as well. Kipsee continued to bark, and sounds of laughter and singing floated out from inside the house. Enticing aromas of nutmeg and cloves filled the air.

A knot formed in the pit of her stomach. The letter and the money must have fallen out when she was wrestling with that horrid boy in the delivery truck. Now what could she do? She drew in a deep breath. "May I see Mr. Patton, please? I've come to interview for the job."

The black man shook his head again. "I don't know. The Mister and Missus has company, and probably don't want no disturbing this evening. Why don't you just come back in the daytime?"

Daytime? Tomorrow? Without money, there was no way Tessa could pay to stay at the YWCA; and even if she had money, she wasn't sure her strength could hold out.

"I've come a long way." She attempted to make her frozen face give him a smile. "I didn't plan to arrive at this time of night—it just happened. I'm sure the interview wouldn't take long. The position's still open, isn't it?"

"Yes'm it is. They be needing a nanny for a month or more."

"Then please..."

"Pole," a gruff voice sounded from inside. "What in thunderation's going on out there? It feels like you're letting in the entire Arctic Region."

The tall black man looked down at her and winked. "It's someone to see you, Mr. Patton."

"Well, why didn't you say so." Suddenly there appeared at the door a stocky man in a business suit. He wore small eyeglasses, and his dark hair was parted down the middle and slicked back on both sides. When he saw Tessa, he stopped and adjusted the glasses. "Who is this child, Pole. Is she begging? Give her something and send her on her way."

"Not begging, sir. She come to talk about being the tutor."

Mr. Patton studied her again. "I'm not hiring a child to teach my children."

Tessa straightened. "Sir, I apologize for arriving so late. I had a problem on the way. I'm nineteen years old, and I've taught school in near the Glenn Pool for a year and a half. May I come in for an interview, please?"

"How do I know you're telling the truth? There's a vast array of riffraff in the city these days." Mr. Patton squinted at her as though to see her a little better.

"You can call Mr. Hargis at Hargis Mercantile near the Glenn Pool. He can vouch for me. He's a member of the school board."

Mr. Patton pulled at his golden watch fob, drew out his watch and snapped it open. "Not likely any store would be open at this hour. Does this school board member have a telephone in his house?"

Tessa shook her head. "No sir. Only at the store." She could see he didn't believe her.

"Anybody else in that place have a telephone where I could call them and ask about you?"

"No sir." Pastor had told no one else but Mr. Hargis. He said the fewer who knew about her leaving, the easier it would be once Papa and Hod learned the truth.

Mr. Patton looked around just as Pole had done, searching to see where she'd come from. When he saw nothing, he looked sternly at her. "You come back tomorrow when I'm not busy. When this Mr. Hargis is at his store, then we can talk business. I'm entertaining guests just now."

Tessa felt the breath go out of her. It was no use. There was nothing more she could do. She turned to go, tearing herself away from that warm doorway, and the splendid aroma of spices and cedar. Back out into the sleet storm, and then where? She had no idea.

As she stepped down the brick steps she forgot about the ice. The last thing she remembered was the feeling of her feet flying upward, the bags scattering, and white-hot searing pain shooting up through her head.

Chapter 5

Warmth. A delicious sensation. She'd been cold for so long. She wanted to open her eyes but couldn't. She moved ever so slightly, but the pain behind her eyes forced her to lie still. Where was she?

"You just be still a mite longer, Honey," came a gentle voice through the fuzziness.

Tessa tried to lift her head, then she realized there was a cloth over her eyes.

"Now Honey, I done told you to be still." A soft hand patted her shoulder. "Goodness you're a tiny little bit of a thing. And you try to tell Mr. Patton you was almost growed? No wonder he don't believe you." There was a chuckle.

"But I am," she protested. With another bit of effort she reached up to pull the cloth from her eyes. She lay on a bed in a small bedroom. Beside the bed was a hefty black woman in a starched white dress, sitting in a straight-back chair. Tessa's cloth coat was draped over the back of a rocking chair which stood in the corner next to a marble-topped bureau.

Tessa squinted against the brightness, then glanced at the ceiling. There was an electrical light fixture. She'd never been in a house with electricity. "Who are you?" she asked. "And where am I?"

"Mr. Patton may be gruff and impatient, but he ain't cruel. He had Pole bring you up here to the apartment over the garage. And I'm Chloe. I cook for the family." Her round face beamed with a friendly smile. "Cooking and what all else they say to do."

Tessa lifted her head to look around, but a fresh jab of pain stopped her. She gave a gasp and let her head fall back.

"You just won't listen, will you? You had a mean whomp on your head, and you needs to be still till you be better."

"How long?"

"Mr. Patton say to let you stay the night anyhow."

Tessa couldn't help but smile. Pastor Stedman always said the Lord worked in strange ways. This was certainly strange.

"Now what you be smiling about? You out in the cold all alone and then you takes a terrible fall on those bricks."

"I just needed a little time, and the Lord seems to have provided it. By tomorrow, Mr. Patton can call and get my recommendation." It even hurt to talk.

Chloe shook her head. "That don't mean he's gonna take you on. Mr. Patton's mighty particular."

"I'm a good teacher," Tessa told her. "And I need this job." But she knew Chloe was right. Just because she was in for the night, didn't mean she had the job. But at least she had a better chance. "'Sufficient unto the day is the evil thereof,'" she quoted. "So for now I'll let tomorrow take care of itself."

Chloe patted her again. "You sure knows your scripture, bless your little heart. And you're exactly right. Ain't no use worrying about things just now. Your bags be setting out in the other room. You needs to sleep, and you'll be perky as can be in the morning. I told you my name, but I clean forgot my manners about asking yours."

"I'm Tessa Jurgen."

Chloe stood to go. "Tessa? Okay, Miss Tessa, when you feel like getting up in the morning, you come in the back door. Go down the hall to the left and when you can't go no further, there be a swinging door, and that's the kitchen. You come on in and I'll fix you breakfast before you talk to Mr. Patton."

"Thank you very much."

"For now, I left crackers, cheese and fruit on a tray out in the living room. Thought you might need a little something tonight as well. Sleep good."

"Chloe?" Tessa clenched her teeth and rose up on one elbow. "Who lives here? Whose place am I in?"

Chloe smiled her nice wide smile. "This here's the garage apartment where the nanny lives."

Tessa thought that's what she would say. She smiled again and lay back down. Surely the Lord wouldn't have put her here tonight if He didn't plan for her to have the position.

Chloe shook her head and another chuckle came from her throat. "You sure be a strange little thing. Mind that ice on the walkway when you come across in the morning. Don't want you to have another crack on that noggin of yours." She pulled the door closed and went out. Tessa heard her steps down the stairway, then heard the door at the bottom of the stairs open and close. All was quiet except for the faint sounds of music wafting over from the big house.

Tessa reached up to feel the lump on the back of her head, and winced. It would be sore for a day or two. Mustering her strength, she rose to her feet. Stepping to the door, she pushed in the bottom button of a wall switch and the lights in the fixture went off. She pushed the top button and they came back on again. Amazing.

A wooden table stood in the center of the living room surrounded by matching chairs. Beneath was a lovely flowered rug. She made it to one of the chairs, but her strength was spent. From where she sat she could see there was a bathroom, and a tiny kitchen. She longed to explore every nook and cranny.

If the quarters for the hired help were this nice, Tessa could scarcely imagine what the big house must be like.

She lifted the cloth off the tray. After eating two crackers, a piece of cheese and half an apple, she knew she must get back to the bed.

With all her heart she wanted to pull her long flannel nightgown from out of the satchel, put it on and crawl between the sheets of the bed. But this place was not hers. Not yet anyway. So she lay down on top the covers and spread the quilt, folded at the foot of the bed, over her. Wind whistled around the little apartment and sleet pelted the windows. Just before falling asleep, she remembered to mumble her thanks to the Lord for this safe haven.

THE NEXT MORNING, SHE was more than careful as she made her way across the icy walkway from the garage to the house. The sleet had stopped, but it was very cold and still. The leaden gray skies threatened to let loose any minute.

Chloe didn't say to knock or to pull the cord. Feeling like an intruder, Tessa left her bags inside the back door and made her way to the kitchen just as she'd been instructed.

As she pushed open the swinging door, she saw Chloe standing at a butcher's block cutting biscuits from thick white dough. The kitchen was quite warm and smelled of sizzling ham. Chloe glanced up. "My, my. What an early bird. It's barely six thirty. The mister won't be down to breakfast for a time yet, so you can eat before you talk to him."

"Thank you, Chloe. May I help you?"

"Just sit yourself down." She pointed to a small table off to the side of the large roomy kitchen. "Nobody'd like it much if I was letting guests help with the cooking and fetching."

"I don't feel like a guest."

"Still..." Chloe swung the large pan of biscuits around and opened a wide oven door and popped them in. "How's the bunged-up head?"

Tessa took off her coat. The room was terribly warm. "Better. And I slept sound. You sure I can't help?" She wasn't used to having someone wait on her.

Chloe poured a glass of milk and set before her. "Nope. Just eat." Next came a hot biscuit, a bowl of gravy with a silver ladle, and two slices of pink ham. The aroma was heavenly. She ate without talking. Chloe never slowed her pace for a moment. Presently a bell rang. "There they be," she announced. She loaded a large tray and went out the door opposite the one Tessa had entered.

When Chloe returned, Tessa carried her plate over to the work area. "If Mr. Patton won't hire me as the tutor, perhaps he would consider hiring me to work in here with you. It looks like you could use help."

Chloe took the plate from her, and gave her a strange look. "Who you fooling?"

"Fooling? No one. I'm going to need a job, somewhere."

"This be black folk work, child." Her flour-spotted dark hand waved around to take in the massive kitchen area. "Ain't nobody gonna take on a white girl to do this." She turned her attention back to the stove. "And you can't work downstairs with Finney and Elsie Mae neither."

"What's downstairs?"

"That's where they do all the laundry and the ironing. Big washing machines and drying lines down there."

"But it's only housework. I've done it all my life."

"Ooh, honey. You gots a lot to learn. I hope you don't get in no trouble before you do."

"What kind of trouble?"

"Where you from, Miss Tessa?"

"On the other side of the Glen Pool."

"I bet you never been around no black folk before."

"A few."

Chloe nodded.

"Just what I thought."

The insistent ringing of the bell interrupted them, Chloe loaded another tray and went out the door. When she returned, she announced that Mr. Patton wanted to see Tessa in the library. Suddenly the food in Tessa's stomach settled down like an anvil.

"You're at the back of the house now," Chloe explained, "and the library is on the second floor in the front of the house. It faces down the draw and out over the river—so's the mister can keep an eye on all his black gold on the west side."

"You mean the refineries?"

"I mean them refineries." She gave a wry smile. "Won't buy him no ticket to heaven but he seem to be happy with things the way they is." Chloe explained which hallway to take and where to turn, but Tessa was thoroughly confused. "You'll find it," she said with a confident wave of her hand.

With that, Tessa found herself once again in the back hall. She smoothed the skirt of her blue print dress. In spite of the fact that the dress was lovingly sewn by Mama, it suddenly seemed plain and common in this setting.

The dark wood in the long hallway gleamed as though each piece had been polished by hand. It gave off a deep burgundy glow. With her cloth coat slung over her arm, she made her way down the hall. Presently she arrived in the massive front entry way with its wide oak door flanked by two narrow windows. The windows were of thick beveled glass with etched floral designs. That was where she stood last evening in the cold, trying to beg the needed interview. The memory of her fall on the bricks made her shudder.

Broad heavy beams crisscrossed on the high ceiling of the foyer. A crystal chandelier hung from the center and to her right a wide staircase beckoned her up to the second floor. She gazed at the tall gaily-decorated Christmas tree, but didn't touch it.

Salmon-colored carpeting softened her steps on the stairs. The banister was of the same rich burgundy wood as that in the hallway.

At the landing there was a set of bay windows where she peered out to view the other magnificent homes lining Galveston Street. None were as large as the Patton mansion, but they were equally beautiful. Pastor had told her there were dozens of millionaires in Tulsa. But until now, it had been a fairy story.

Past the bay windows, and up the next flight of stairs, she was faced with another hallway. The second door, Chloe had said, but was it the right or the left? *Oh Lord, please let me remember.* Later, of course she realized it would have been the left, because Chloe said it faced the front toward the river. But in her nervousness, the right one was the door she chose.

Her hand closed over the cool glass knob, she turned it and the door silently swung open. There before her was a spacious room full of games, toys and bookshelves. Desks were situated by the tall windows. A little girl with long dark curls sat on a rug playing with a doll in a lacy pink dress. An older boy sat astride the largest rocking horse Tessa had ever seen. They looked at her with surprised faces, and the dog, Kipsee, gave a couple of yaps.

A girl who appeared to be sixteen or so, was curled up in a window seat reading a book. She shot Tessa a hate-filled look. "Who are you and what do you want?" she demanded. "What are you doing in our house?" She stood to her feet.

"Excuse me, I was looking for Mr. Patton's library. I have an appointment."

"An appointment for what?" the girl asked. "What business could you possibly have with my father?"

Tessa quickly realized it was not wise to further agitate this girl. She seemed to enjoy being angry. "Where's the library?" she asked.

"Across the hall," the little girl on the floor said kindly.

"Thank you," Tessa answered and quickly closed the door.

It took a moment before she could regain her composure. Such rudeness.

She walked across the wide hall and tapped at the door just to be safe. A deep voice invited her in.

Mr. Patton was sitting behind a heavy oak desk which, as Chloe said, was partially turned so he could look out the floor- to-ceiling windows and see the refineries. In a chair beside the desk sat a prim, buxom woman dressed in a wine-colored silken dress. Her expression of disdain was an exact replica of the young girl's across the hall.

Chapter 6

M r. Patton did not stand, but greeted her in a reserved manner, pointing to a nearby chair. She sat down with her back to the tall windows.

"Now Miss," he said, "we seem to have a bit of unfinished business. Please give me your name again."

"Tessa Jurgen."

"Yes, Miss Jurgen, and how is your head? You took a nasty fall."

Absently, she reached up to touch the bump. "I'm fine, and thank you kindly for letting me stay the night."

He leaned back in his high-back leather swivel chair. "I could hardly send you out in the storm in your condition. Now tell me what it is you wanted?"

Had he forgotten so quickly? "Sir, I'm applying for the position of nanny and tutor for the children. The one listed in the classifieds in the *Tulsa World*."

Mr. and Mrs. Patton exchanged looks. "But you're so young," Mrs. Patton said. Her voice carried a thick drawl of one from the South.

"I may be small, Mrs. Patton, but I'm nineteen, soon to be twenty. I've taught children at the Independence School near the Glenn Pool for three semesters. My students are excelling in their subjects."

Mr. Patton fingered his gold watch fob and gazed past her out the windows. "If you were doing so well, why did you leave?"

Tessa paused, unsure of how much she should tell.

"Just as I thought," Mrs. Patton broke in, misunderstanding her hesitation. "You've run away from home and you're making up a story so as to gain employment. Henry, I tried to tell you she's a vagabond. I'm sorry Miss..."

42

"Now Trevalene," Mr. Patton interrupted, "remain calm. I'll handle this."

Tessa could hardly believe this woman would think her a liar. "I tried to explain last evening. I had a letter of recommendation from one of the school board members, but there was a..." What could she say about her incident with Jack? "There was a mishap and it must have fallen from my pocket. The letter was signed by Pastor Stedman and Mr. Clyde Hargis. Pastor doesn't have a phone, but Mr. Hargis has one at the Mercantile Store. If you call him he'll tell you."

"I'm sure you realize this storm has caused problems with the phone lines. There may not even be a connection that far from Tulsa."

"Of course she knows, Henry. Let her go. She's probably not even qualified to deal with our children."

Tessa leaned forward in her chair. "If you're indicating they may be more difficult than the children of the roughnecks and roustabouts in the oil field, then perhaps you're right."

Trevalene Patton gave a slight gasp. "Wesley is nothing akin to those ruffians. But he's nearly as tall as you are."

"What does size matter? I trust you've taught him to respect any person you set in charge over him, no matter the size."

"The girl has a point, Trevalene." Mr. Patton straightened his eyeglasses and looked right at Tessa as though to look inside her. Though it made her tense, she met his gaze. He rolled the leather chair to reach for the pedestal phone on his desk and made a few clicks. "Operator? Can we get through to the Glenn Pool? Well, give it a try. Get me the Hargis Mercantile Store."

Silently Tessa pray for the call to go through. She waited through the uncomfortable quiet.

"Plenty of static, that's for sure." Mr. Patton turned to look out the tall windows. "It's snowing," he announced.

Tessa twisted around to look. The flakes were fat and full. The tall windows gave a panoramic view down the hill and out across the river.

The day was so gray, one could barely make out the bank on the far side of the Arkansas.

"It's ringing," he said.

Tessa's heart jumped. *Lord, please...*

"Hargis Mercantile? Yes, I'm calling for Clyde Hargis, this is Henry Patton in Tulsa." He lowered the phone. "They're calling him. Terrible static. Can hardly hear."

Tessa twisted her hands tightly together beneath her folded coat.

Mr. Patton lifted the phone again. "Mr. Hargis, there's a young lady, a Miss Tessa Jurgen, in my home who tells me you can give her a recommendation as a tutor. Says she had a letter of recommendation but somehow it was lost. Excuse me?" His voice rose louder. "Lost. Yes, the letter is lost. What do you say to that? What? Can you speak louder Mr. Hargis? I can barely hear you." After a pause, he answered. "Yes, yes, I see. Very well. Thank you."

"Was I right?" asked Mrs. Patton.

"No, my dear, you were wrong. I could barely hear Mr. Hargis, but I did hear him clearly say that Miss Jurgen here is an excellent instructor, has a high level of integrity and is a good Christian girl. He'll be sending along a new copy of the letter next week."

Tessa felt her body go limp. Finally.

"But, Henry, I'm still not sure..."

"My dear, I'll make the decisions around here." Mr. Patton hooked the receiver and set the phone down. "Miss Jurgen, we are in dire need of a competent tutor and nanny and I'd like to offer you the position. It pays twenty dollars a week. You'll have private quarters in the apartment where you spent the night."

Ah the beautiful little apartment with electric lights and running water. Tessa could hardly believe it. Twenty dollars a week. At the Independence School, she made thirty dollars a month. Now she'd be a greater help to Mama than ever.

"You'll have Saturday afternoons and Sundays off. You will lunch with the children on school days, and have breakfast and dinner in your own apartment. Is that suitable?"

"Yes sir. Thank you, sir."

"Now I suggest you go back to the apartment, get settled in, and rest today. Since we are still in the holiday week, you won't be doing much until after the New Year. We can talk more tomorrow. Do you have any questions?"

"Yes, sir. Please tell me about the children. How many are there?"

"We have three children," Mrs. Patton broke in to answer. "But you'll deal only with Wesley, who's ten, and Lucie who's seven. Our older daughter, Sadella, is sixteen. She'll be leaving to return to boarding school next week."

Tessa gave another inward sigh of relief.

"Henry," Mrs. Patton addressed her husband. "This girl has no clothes. She can't possibly accompany us about town in what she's wearing."

Mr. Patton waved his hand as though it were of precious little importance. "So buy her an outfit. And especially a warm coat." He was now leafing through several papers on his desk and didn't look up.

As Mrs. Patton rose, her silken dress made a soft swishing sound. "Use this morning to unpack your things, Miss Jurgen. You may eat lunch in the breakfast room. Chloe will fix you something. Then meet me in the back drive at three. We'll motor into Tulsa and see if we can find you a few things."

"Trevalene, not today for land's sake. It's snowing outside."

"All the more reason to quickly purchase her a decent coat."

In some things, Mrs. Patton did have the last say. Tessa wanted to argue that she needed no one to buy her clothes, but it certainly wasn't the time to fuss. She stood and followed Mrs. Patton out the door and into the hallway.

"I'll introduce you to the children before you leave." She crossed the hall and opened the opposite door. "Children," she said as she ushered Tessa inside, "I'd like to introduce your new tutor and nanny."

"She's not mine." The girl in the window seat spoke but didn't bother to look up from the book she was reading.

"I don't want a boring old tutor," Wesley protested. He dismounted the large horse and went to the corner and picked up a metal top and made it spin. It created a high melodic whine as the designs blurred while it turned. "I want to go to Riverview School with the guys up the street."

Lucie was the only one who showed any interest or respect. She came running over with the porcelain doll in the crook of her arm. Looking up at Tessa, she smiled and said, "Hello. I'm Lucie." She primly extended her hand.

"I'm so pleased to meet you, Lucie." Tessa shook her warm little hand.

"And this," she said, holding up the doll, "is Sophia. Santa Claus brought her to me for Christmas."

"Hello to you, Sophia." Tessa shook the doll's hand, and Lucie giggled. The exquisite doll had perfect cupid-bow lips, pink cheeks, and wide dark eyes that looked as real as Lucie's. From beneath the ribboned lace hat hung shining gold ringlets. The beauty of the doll fascinated Tessa.

"Wesley." Mrs. Patton spoke with a new firmness. "Come here."

The boy gave the top a kick to prove his reluctance and stomped across the room.

"Wesley, this is Miss Tessa Jurgen. You will be getting acquainted with her this week, and your studies will begin on Monday."

Tessa shook Wesley's limp unwilling hand. In spite of his rudeness, she almost felt sorry for him.

"Sadella, mind your manners and come greet Miss Jurgen."

Sadella's eyes were riveted on the page, her pinched, narrow face remained a mask. "She's not my nanny."

"No one said she was." There was a pause. "Sadella, I'm waiting. Shall I call your father from his office?"

With a slam of the book, Sadella stood. One day this girl would be willowy, but for now she was gangly—all arms and legs. Her hair was bobbed and styled in soft waves about her face, with one severe curl pressed in the center of her forehead. She stood nearly six inches taller than Tessa. Her handshake was as stiff as Wesley's was limp. Her words were equally stiff. "Hello, Miss Jurgen. Good luck with these two. You'll need it."

"Hello, Sadella. How kind of you to wish me good luck."

"The girls at school call me Sadie. I hate the name Sadella." She shot a look toward her mother.

"Sadella was your grandmother's given name. A name you should be proud of."

"It's old fashioned."

Mrs. Patton did not encourage the argument, but turned to leave, motioning Tessa toward the door. In the hall, she said, "Remember, Miss Jurgen, three o'clock. Don't be tardy. I cannot abide tardiness."

"I'll be ready." As Tessa moved down the hall, she heard Wesley say, "You're going downtown? May we go, too?" Tessa was too far down the hall to hear the answer, but she hoped Mrs. Patton said no.

Before lunch time had arrived, Tessa's few belonging were neatly put away, and there was time to pen a note to Pastor and Edith. Hopefully they would take the news of her whereabouts to Mama and the girls. It didn't seem right that Mama still thought she was with Pastor when she was actually miles away. It was like living a lie. But what she was to do about Papa not knowing was a total mystery.

Through the morning, the snow piled up in soft drifts. When she stepped outside her doorway to cross to the big house for lunch, a walkway had been shoveled clear. She draped her muffler loosely over her head.

Inside the kitchen, Chloe stirred a mammoth black kettle on the stove filled with simmering vegetable soup. The aroma filled the room. Pots, pans and every imaginable utensil hung from racks above Chloe's head. At the corner table sat a lean black boy who was already devouring a big bowl of the soup.

Chloe turned around when she heard the door, and gave her bright smile. "Hey, child. Let me guess. You been hired?"

"You guessed right. Mr. Patton made the needed phone call, and thank the Lord, in spite of the storm, the call went through."

"I have a place set for you in the breakfast room, Honey. I'm fixing you hot soup and a big old mug of hot cocoa. How's that sound?"

"Heavenly."

"Mm hm, I thought so."

Tessa pulled off her coat and muffler and placed it on the chair opposite the boy. "And who's this? We've not met."

"That's my son, Jasper. He's one smart boy. Gone all the way to the twelfth grade at Booker T. Washington High. Gonna graduate in May. We so proud of him. He been out there shoveling snow all morning."

"You're the one who provided a path for me. I'm pleased to meet you Jasper."

Jasper barely looked up, but gave a slight nod.

Tessa pulled out the chair. "I hope you don't mind if I join you. I hate to eat alone."

As she started to sit down, the boy jumped to his feet. "No ma'am. You can't do that," he said, eyes wide.

"He's right, child. You can't sit there with him. I got your place set out here in pretty blue breakfast nook just like Mrs. Patton done told me."

"But what's wrong with right here? No need to dirty up another place."

Chloe put down her large stirring spoon and walked over to the table. "Honey, don't you know you can't be sitting with no black folk? Mercy to goodness, if the Missus take a notion to stick her head in here and see Jasper eating with you, she'd have our heads for sure. Now you don't want that, do you?"

"What a silly notion. Pastor Stedman says God created everyone alike, so what makes the difference?"

Chloe wiped her hands on her white apron. "Your Pastor what's-his-name must not live in Tulsa. In Tulsa, it make a whopping big difference. You gots a lot to learn, child."

Tessa heaved a big sigh. "Yes, I suppose I do. But I don't have to like it do I?"

"We don't even think about whether we likes it—that's the way things is."

Looking up at the tall slender boy, Tessa said, "Please sit down and finish your soup while it's still hot. I'll go to the breakfast nook. But I'm sure I'd enjoy lunch with you."

The boy returned her smile. His face was as gentle as his mother's. "Thank you very much, ma'am." But he remained standing until Chloe had led Tessa out the other door, down the hall to the breakfast nook. There she ate alone, watching delicate flakes dancing outside the bay windows. In spite of the indifference of Wesley and the antagonism from Sadella, she was grateful for the hot food, and her new warm home.

Later in her apartment, she took out her knitting and worked on the stockings as she prayed about the dreaded shopping trip. At a quarter till three, she heard the garage door open followed by a motor starting. She pulled on her coat and draped her muffler over her head then watched out the window.

The tall black man, named Pole, whom she now knew as Chloe's cousin, was driving the car. As it backed into the wide drive between the garage and the house, Tessa could see it was a Willys-Knight touring car. She sucked in her breath. She'd seen pictures of that expensive car in Edith's issues of Saturday Evening Post. Never did she ever dream she would ride in one. She went downstairs and waited by the back door of the house.

When Mrs. Patton came out, a sullen Sadella followed close behind her. Both wore heavy coats with thick fur collars. Sadella's hands were concealed in a matching fur muff hung about her neck. She didn't look at Tessa as she reached up to adjust her close-fitting fur hat before climbing into the car.

Pole then assisted Mrs. Patton in, and her broad-brimmed dark hat barely cleared the top of the door. Awkwardly, Tessa allowed Pole to assist her into the seat beside Mrs. Patton.

She tried not to gawk, but this was nothing like Pastor's Model T. The interior of the car was as warm as her apartment. Plush blue carpet felt springy beneath her feet, and the mohair upholstery was finer than Edith's davenport in the parlor. The motor sounded like the purring of a cat. It was so quiet, Tessa could hardly believe it was running. As the car moved down the gently sloping drive and out onto Galveston Street, she watched carefully to make mental notes of each street.

"I don't want to go back on Friday," Sadella was saying to her mother. "Why do I have to go back? Tulsa High School is one of the best schools in the country. I can get everything I need right here."

"Except exposure, my dear. There's no need for you to be associating with all the riffraff that happens to fall into this town."

"But mother..."

"It's settled, Sadella." To close the subject further, Mrs. Patton turned to Tessa. "Wesley can't seem to grasp his multiplication tables, Miss Jurgen. I'm not sure where the trouble lies."

As they approached Elgin, Tessa saw this was the street where the trolley ran. She would need to know that later on.

"He excels in reading," Mrs. Patton continued, "and all he wants to do is read stories. You will need to set arithmetic as the utmost importance and see to it that he knows all the tables by spring."

"Yes, ma'am. We'll have no trouble with it, I'm sure."

Downtown was a glittering array of colored lights sparkling everywhere. Store windows vied for the grandest display of goods. How Tessa wished Vega and Siegrid could see this.

"To Vandever's, Pole."

"Yes'm."

Some of the buildings were many stories high. Tessa tried counting, but lost track. More than twelve. One could get sick riding an elevator to the top.

Pole pulled the touring car right up to the front door of the department store then stepped out to open the door for them. "I've several items to purchase for Sadella before she returns to boarding school, Miss Jurgen." Mrs. Patton led the way into the store, and Tessa could hardly hear her. "Please stay here in the main part of the store until I come down for you. I'll try to find you a suitable coat before we leave. Browse if you like, but please don't stray far."

As they turned to leave, Sadella turned back to Tessa and mouthed the words, "...don't stray far," and shook her finger.

Tessa chose to ignore the rebellious child. Mrs. Patton certainly had her hands full with that one. Tessa was much too preoccupied looking at all the things in the store to care about the silly actions of a spoiled rich girl.

She moved about looking at the displays, and pulled the muffler from her head letting it fall around her shoulders. Absently, she touched her braids to see if they were firmly in place, and tucked in a few loose wisps.

She came to a glass case full of gold watches. There were ladies watches that hung from decorative pendants. The covers were etched with fine carvings. How delicate they looked.

"Excuse me," came a male voice from beside her. "Would your name by any chance be Jurgen?"

Startled, Tessa turned and looked up into the cool blue eyes of a young man, bundled up in a tweed overcoat. When he tipped his hat, she could see his hair was the color of her own. "How could you possibly know my name?" she asked.

"Tessa, don't you recognize your own cousin? I'm Erik Torsten, the youngest of your Uncle Artur's boys."

"Erik? My gracious. What are you doing in Tulsa? I thought you lived in Bartlesville."

"I came to attend Kendall College, but the war changed all that. I'm trying to finish now."

"We heard you were in the war. Mama made Papa bring us into town when all the soldiers came home. But it was so crowded, Papa refused to stay long enough for her to find you. She cried on the way home."

Her broad-shouldered cousin reached out and touched her shoulder. "Sounds like your Papa is as cantankerous as ever."

"That's not even the half of it. But it's not important. How on earth did you recognize me?"

A soft blush colored Erik's fair cheeks. "First of all, you look like Grandma Torsten—so tiny all her life. But the braids gave you away. Looks just like Grandma and your aunties." He paused. "Not many women wear braids these days."

Tessa hadn't even thought about her hair not being in style. She quickly glanced around and Erik was right. No one wore braids anymore. She thought of Sadella's bobbed hair and stylish waves.

"But I still like long hair," Erik said with a teasing smile, "and I think your braids are beautiful."

"You think *what's* beautiful, Torsten?" Another male voice sounded behind her.

"Oh Tessa," Erik said, "I'd like you to meet my old war buddy, and fellow boarding house compatriot..."

Tessa turned to see the wide smile and the shining dark eyes she'd seen the night before. He stood just a bit shorter than Erik, but ramrod straight.

"His name is Gaven MacIntyre."

Chapter 7

Gaven's eyes were wide with surprise. "You! The little runaway girl." He snatched off his hat before reaching out to grasp her hand.

"You two know each other?"

"I tried to tell you," Tessa said to the man in defense, "I'm not a little girl, nor a runaway." But now she was embarrassed that she'd been so rude to him. She hoped the heat she felt in her cheeks didn't show.

"I'm relieved to see you're all right. I was worried sick half the night wondering if you were safe."

"What's this all about, Mac?" Erik broke in.

"I borrowed Mike's roadster last evening to run back to Riverview. I'd forgotten to pick up a set of papers that needed grading before the holiday is out. This little lady was walking all alone on Riverside in a sleet storm."

Erik turned to her. "Alone in the storm? In Tulsa? Your Mama would never allow..."

"I know it sounds terrible, but really, I did have a ride to the Patton's. Or so I thought." She took in a breath. How was she supposed to know how much to tell? If Erik were alone, perhaps she might explain the whole mess about Hod, since he understood about Papa. "It's such a long story."

"At least tell us why you were going to the Patton mansion, of all places," Erik said.

But before she could explain, she heard Trevalene Patton calling. "Miss Jurgen? Miss Jurgen? Oh, there you are." She strode toward them with Sadella close behind. "I thought I told you not to stray, and here you are talking to two strange men."

Tessa opened her mouth to say she hadn't *strayed* at all, when Erik spoke up. "Good afternoon, Mrs. Patton. It's good to see you again. I've not visited with you since I covered the fund raiser you organized for the Ecumenic Club."

"Excuse me?" Mrs. Patton stopped and looked at Erik more closely. "Ah, the young man who reported the story for the World. I didn't recognize you for a moment. You did a fine job on that article. A fine job."

Gaven waved toward Tessa. "And Miss Jurgen here is Erik's cousin."

Mrs. Patton raised her brows momentarily. "I see." She turned to Gaven. "And who might you be?"

Gaven stretched out his hand. "Gaven MacIntyre, ma'am. Erik and I were war buddies. Now we live in the same boarding house. I teach sixth grade at Riverview School."

"Wesley wants to go to Riverview," Sadella put in, though no one had addressed her. The comment was ignored.

Mrs. Patton turned again to Erik. "I suppose your young cousin explained that she is now in our employ."

"No ma'am, we hadn't gotten that far."

"Miss Jurgen, we really must go now. If you will please come along."

"I'll be right there," Tessa said. "I'd like another word with my cousin if you don't mind."

Mrs. Patton paused. "I suppose. But please make it quick." As they stepped away, Sadella gave Gaven a coy smile.

"Does Mrs. Patton always talk to you like that?" Gaven asked.

"I'm not sure. This is my first day."

"You should talk." Erik elbowed his friend. "You're the one who thought she was a little girl."

"Yeah, but that biddy knows better—I didn't know."

Tessa tried to stifle a giggle. "She is rather stuffy."

Gaven shook his head. "That's an understatement."

"Just keep in mind," Erik told her, "she was living in a shotgun house before the old man struck oil. Now she's in every civic club, and on every committee in Tulsa. What is it you're doing for them?"

"Nanny and tutor for the two younger children."

"Tutor?" Gaven's dark eyes lit up with interest. "You're a teacher?" Each time he spoke, he seemed to move closer.

"I taught at a little country school is all. I took the county exam." Though she was proud of her work at Independence, she knew it was nothing in comparison to the sophisticated school system of Tulsa. Gaven no doubt had his degree.

"I bet your students loved you."

The burning in her cheeks flared again under the scrutiny of Gaven's sincere eyes. "I pray they did. I certainly loved them."

Erik pushed his hat to the back of his head. "Word has it that young Wesley Patton is quite a young rebel."

"I've heard that too," Gaven agreed glancing over at Erik. "But I bet Tessa here can handle him."

"Time will tell," she offered, still somewhat flustered by his comments.

"Here's my address, and the phone number at the boarding house," Erik told her as he pulled a small pad and a stub of a pencil from his coat pocket, and began scribbling. "And also the number at the *Tulsa World*. I'm a reporter there. Call if you need anything."

She nodded and started to go.

"Erik," Gaven said, nudging his friend. "What about Friday night?" He glanced at Tessa and back at Erik.

Erik nodded. "Oh yeah. Say Tessa, our church is having a New Year's watch Friday night. It would be nice to have you come. Will you have New Year's Eve off?"

"I'm not sure, but I think so. I don't begin teaching until Monday."

Gaven was looking at her again. "A bunch of us could come by at eight," he said, giving her his captivating smile. "Someone always has a car available. Where shall we pick you up?"

When Tessa lived with Pastor and Edith, she always turned to them to ask permission, but now she would be making decisions on her own. What an odd sensation. "I'm in the garage apartment behind the house. But I'll wait at the back gate at eight."

"Splendid." Gaven reached out to take her hand and held it for an endless moment. "I'm pleased to have met you—and to learn that you survived the stormy night."

"Thank you." As she pulled loose, she felt her heart racing. "I really must go. Good-by Gaven, Erik."

She hurried to where Mrs. Patton was waiting at the elevator. "It's about time," her employer said curtly.

But Tessa barely heard her. She was thrilled to know her own cousin lived right here in Tulsa. But more than that, Gaven's gentle, but persistent attention had warmed her heart. She followed Mrs. Patton and Sadella into the elevator. "Third floor," Mrs. Patton instructed the elevator operator.

The dreaded fitting session was now tempered by her pleasant experience. Mrs. Patton's way of treating her like a child didn't even matter. Tessa's new coat was forest green with black velvet piping trim and collar. The lining was black and silky. It fit perfectly and felt snug and warm. Tessa was certain it cost a fortune, and had no idea how she would pay the money back.

She wore the coat home and over her arm she carried the old black one that Mama had sewed for her. She would pack it away. It would still be a good coat for early next spring.

That evening, Chloe had a tray ready for Tessa's supper, and suggested she take it up to her apartment to eat. It seemed a better idea than the breakfast nook. Tessa looked forward to receiving her first pay envelope—then she could buy her own groceries.

Before taking her heavy-laden tray, Tessa modeled her new coat for Chloe. "Mmm hmm," she grunted in approval. "Now don't you look mighty classy in that number. No more half-frozen little girl now. The missus like her people to look nice. Yes, she does."

"But the coat isn't the best part," Tessa told her. "I ran into my own cousin. My mother's brother's son. His name is Erik. I've not seen him for years."

"Now ain't that nice? Family right here in Tulsey town. What a blessed girl you are."

"He introduced me to a friend of his who served with him in the war. They've invited me to a New Year's Eve watch night at their church."

Chloe turned from the meat she was cutting. "Ah hum. Is that a twinkle I see in your blue eye? What's this *friend* like?"

Tessa plunged her hands into the deep silky pockets of her coat and shrugged her shoulders. "I just met him. All I know is he lives in a boarding house with Erik, and he teaches sixth grade at a school called Riverview."

Chloe pointed the knife in her hand. "Riverview be just up the road a bit toward town. Nice school."

"He has laughing brown eyes, and a nice smile."

"Sound mighty good to me," Chloe said with a chuckle.

"Is it all right if I go? I mean, do I need to ask the Pattons for permission?"

Chloe laughed out loud. "Oh child, you is from the country. What you do on your own time is your business. They may hire you, but they don't own you. New Year's Eve ain't in working hours. You go on and have a nice time."

That was just what Tessa needed to hear. "Thanks, I will." She picked up her tray to go. "One more thing, Chloe. Is Wesley a rebel?"

"No more than any other ten-year-old who been given everything he want, every day of his life. I'll wager you tangled with a rebel or two at that country school. But this here's a spoiled boy who gets his own way too much of the time."

Tessa nodded. "I thought so."

"I'll tell you something else." The words were punctuated with the waving of the butcher knife. "I'd as soon tangle with Wesley any day as with that gal, Sadella."

Remembering the young girl's mocking face at Vandever's, Tessa could almost agree. "I wonder why she's so full of hate."

"Some of us knows why." Chloe's voice went soft.

Tessa stepped closer. "Is it something terrible?"

Chloe shook her head and made a clucking sound in her throat. "Her mama don't have no use for her. Cause of the way she was born."

Tessa thought a moment. "Out of wedlock?"

Chloe returned to methodically cutting the meat. In the quiet, Tessa wasn't sure the black woman was even going to answer the question. Then she nodded. "Yep. And that was bad enough for all the shame of a fine girl from the South, but that ain't all."

Tessa shifted her weight to the other foot. The heavy coat was becoming quite warm, but she didn't move. "What happened with Sadella, Chloe?"

"Miss Trevalene's mama done put her out when they find out she was in the family way. Here she was a mere bit of a girl, fixing to have a baby and nowhere to go. My Great Aunt Teppy and a friend of hers found Miss Trevalene in a old barn. She woulda bled plumb to death. They carried her to Aunt Teppy's house, and sent for the black doctor. He delivered baby Sadella. Missus Trevalene Patton had growed up not liking us blacks very much. Instead of being obliged, that seemed to make her worse. The shame of it all. Don't know that many white folk know the story, and no black in Tulsey Town would breathe a word of it. Not now anyhow."

"And Mr. Patton?"

"He was just a small-town merchant. Owned a hardware store just over there on Detroit Avenue. He gets word about the whole mess and takes pity on her. Marries her real fast like, and takes in the baby. A year or so later, he pours all his money in oil drilling and you knows the rest."

"Does Sadella know?"

Chloe shook her black curls again. "I ain't sure. If I was betting, I'd bet not."

Tessa could hardly imagine a mother hating her child because of how she was born. It didn't make much sense. And now she could almost feel sorry for Sadella. Still, she was thankful the elder Patton child was leaving on the train Thursday afternoon.

Saying good-night to Chloe, Tessa backed out of the kitchen door with the tray in her hands. When she turned around, she caught sight of Sadella slipping away down the hall.

Chapter 8

That evening Tessa took a hot bath in the tub, which stood on ball and claw legs in the tiled bathroom. Hot water without carrying heavy scalding kettles from the wood stove—what a heavenly blessing. She didn't even mind that the Arkansas River offered mud and grit in the water as well. How she wished Mama could enjoy this kind of luxury.

As Tessa fell asleep that evening, she was giddy with excitement thinking of the New Year's Eve party. And in her mind's eye, she saw the smiling face of Gaven MacIntyre.

THE SUN WAS SHINING brightly on the new snow on Thursday morning. The whiteness almost blinded Tessa as she walked over to the big house. This would be her first time alone with the children. She was to spend the morning with them while Mrs. Patton and Sadella went on another shopping expedition downtown. Orders were for her to report to the "children's room" at nine, which is what they called the room with all the toys, the bookshelves and the inviting window seat. When she opened the door, she was met first by Kipsee, the white terrier. He gave a few little yips, danced around Tessa's feet, then paused to allow her to pat his silky head.

Lucie was seated on the oval carpet near the tall windows. She looked up from playing with Sophia. Tessa sensed the girl wanted to come to her, but instead, Lucie stared at her brother who was playing with toy airplanes in the corner.

"Good morning," she greeted them. "And hello to you, Kipsee."

"I think he likes you," Lucie said in a soft voice, again glancing over at Wesley.

"No, he doesn't," Wesley stated. "Here, Kipsee. Come here boy." The dog obeyed, scattering the toy airplanes Wesley had lined in a neat row. "No. Don't mess up my game. Bad dog."

Tessa knelt down on the rug beside Lucie. "How's Sophia this morning? Has she had breakfast?"

Lucie's face beamed. Tessa could tell she enjoyed make believe. "Yes, she's had her breakfast, and I'm putting her down for her nap."

"A nap? Then perhaps she'd enjoy a story before her nap. Shall we read to her?"

"Oh yes," Lucie agreed quickly. "Sophia just loves stories."

"What story is her favorite? Let's read her favorite."

Lucie thought a moment. She stood and went to the bookshelf and scanned the books. "Mmm, let's see."

"Traitor," Wesley said to his sister in a low voice.

"I am not a traitor," Lucie retorted. "We're just reading to Sophia. There's nothing wrong with that."

Lucie came back with *Pollyanna*, which was one of Tessa's favorites as well.

"Would you like to join us, Wesley?" Tessa asked.

"Play with girls and dolls? Not on your life!"

Tessa pointed to the window seat. "Shall we take Sophia over there and make her more comfortable?"

Gently Lucie lifted the doll from the wicker pram. "Sophia would like that." Lucie snuggled close to Tessa on the brocade pillows arranged in the window seat, and cradled Sophia in her arms. Periodically Lucie arranged and rearranged the doll's soft curls and glossy ribbons.

As Tessa read, Wesley interrupted. "Tomorrow, I'll be playing with all the other boy up the street. I won't need you two."

"Mother says you can't go out and play until the snow melts," Lucie countered. "You might catch the grippe."

Wesley muttered to himself as he again lined up the toy airplanes in a neat row. Tessa continued reading.

"Someday I'm going to own my own airplane," Wesley interrupted again. "I may start my own airline company. Dad says I can learn to fly when I'm old enough."

Again, Tessa began to read and again Wesley interrupted. "When I'm sixteen, Dad's going to give me my first oil well. He's going to teach me all about running it, too."

"Wesley, have you never been taught that it's rude to interrupt? If you want to discuss your future plans, we can talk when I'm finished reading to Lucie."

"Reading to Sophia," Lucie corrected.

"Yes, I mean reading to Sophia."

"That's just a dumb old doll. You're not really reading to the doll. That's faking. And I don't want to talk to you anyway. I don't even want you in this room."

"Sophia isn't a dumb doll, Wesley James Patton," Lucie said. "You take back those words right now."

"I will not."

Tessa ousted Lucie from her lap and walked toward Wesley to confront him. But he pranced about to another part of the room, daring her to follow. If he planned to reduce this to a game of tag, Tessa refused to play. There would be other ways to win him over. For now, she returned to the window seat and continued reading to Lucie. There were a few more interruptions, but she ignored him. Eventually, he tired of the efforts.

By the time Chloe announced lunch, Tessa felt Lucie was now her friend. But time was needed for Wesley.

That afternoon, she was to keep the children "in tow" while she accompanied the family to the Frisco Railroad depot. Sadella's train was scheduled to leave at two-thirty. While Mr. and Mrs. Patton saw about the ticket and the connections, Pole unloaded two steamer trunks and several suitcases from the touring car onto a cart. Tessa marveled that one person could have enough belongings to fill two trunks. Pole rolled the cart into the front door of the station, through the bustling crowd of people, and out the other side to the platform by the tracks.

Lucie held tightly to Tessa's hand. Wesley tried to act as though he didn't even know them. A shrill train whistle sounded in the distance.

"Sadie doesn't want to go," Lucie said with a note of sadness in her voice.

"Your mother wants you to use your sister's full name," Tessa reminded her.

"She still doesn't want to go." Lucie led them to hard wooden benches where they sat down.

Wesley sat opposite them and cupped his chin in his hand, propping his elbow on the arm rest. He was dressed in a proper suit coat which matched his knickers. "I wish it was me getting on that train. I'd want to go for sure. I'd rather go to a boarding school, than have a dumb old nanny. Nannies are for babies."

The whistle sounded again, louder and closer. Mr. and Mrs. Patton came over to where they were sitting. Sadella followed. Her red-rimmed eyes confirmed Lucie's statement. Lucie gave her sister a good-bye hug, but Wesley remained seated. Tessa puzzled at the lack of warmth between them, remembering her close kinship with Berg.

"Keep the children well out of the way, Miss Jurgen. We'll get Sadella settled before she leaves."

"Yes ma'am."

Suddenly, the noise from the incoming train was almost deafening. As it chugged to a halt, Tessa watched Sadella with hunched shoulders following her parents toward the platform. The smell of thick dark smoke filled the station, as passengers moved out toward the train.

"There are postcards on the counter," Lucie said. "May I look?"

"Let's all look. Come on Wesley."

Reluctantly, Wesley followed them to the counter. There were interesting post cards from different places in Oklahoma. There was even one of the great lake of oil and the many derricks at the Glenn Pool. Tessa explained that she had lived near there. Other cards had pictures of pretty ladies with ruffled dresses and parasols. These were Lucie's favorites.

A moment later, when Tessa turned to ask Wesley about his favorite cards, he was gone. Her heart jumped. "Wesley?" Quickly she scanned the room which was now almost empty. Even those who were not boarding were on the platform saying good-bye.

"Where is he, Miss Jurgen? Where'd Wesley go?" Lucie's dark eyes grew large.

"He's probably playing a trick on us," she said forcing calmness into her voice. "He likes tricks doesn't he?"

Lucie nodded, but wasn't totally convinced. "What kind of trick is he playing?"

"I'm not sure, but I'll have to find out. Will you do me a big favor and stay here until I do?" Tessa lifted Lucie into a seat. "Promise to stay?"

"Promise."

Tessa moved to the far end of the station and went out the door. She assumed whatever Wesley was up to, he'd do it as far from his parents as possible. She glanced around at the parked automobiles but saw nothing. Whispering a quick prayer, she started to walk down the length of the train. Surely he wouldn't get on.

"All aboard!" sang out the porter in a deep throaty voice. The whistle echoed the warning. Tessa stepped along more quickly, looking up at the windows as she passed each car. It wouldn't have surprised her a bit to see Wesley's face staring back at her.

Finally, several cars down, she spotted him. He was on the steps leading up to the rear of a passenger car. "Wesley," she called out.

"Yah, yah. You can't catch me. You'll be in trouble now. Mother told you to keep me in tow." He gave a high-pitched, little-boy giggle.

Both anger and fear tasted bitter in her throat. If he were in her classroom, she would have used the willow switch on him. But this was much different than a classroom.

Slowly the wheels began turning. "Yah, yah," Wesley taunted again. "Can't catch me."

She was closer now. "I don't even want to catch you Wesley Patton. As soon as the porter finds you don't have a ticket, you'll be put off quick enough."

"I could buy a ticket," he yelled back. The train was moving now. "Ha! My dad could buy this whole train."

But even as he talked, Tessa could tell he was getting ready to leap off. It was all a show. A spoiled child putting on a big show.

"Be careful," she warned.

He started to jump, but he was caught. Somehow his jacket sleeve was caught. His eyes grew wide and full of fear. "Miss Jurgen, help me, please! I can't get loose!"

Tessa was even with him now. There were patches of snow. She tried not to slip as she ran. Faster. As it came by, her short legs made one giant leap, and she grabbed the rail. She yanked his sleeve as hard as she could, and heard a rip. Together they jumped free and fell into a snow bank.

Miraculously she was unhurt. "Are you all right?" She stood and reached out to help him up.

Wesley only nodded, brushing off his nice clothes.

"Let me look at that sleeve."

He held out his arm. There was a rip and the button on the sleeve was missing.

"Give it to me," she told him.

Without question, he took off the coat. She folded the torn sleeve inside the coat and draped it neatly over her arm. When they returned to Lucie, Mr. and Mrs. Patton were there waiting.

"I thought I told you to keep the children away from the train," Mrs. Patton said.

"Wesley wanted a closer look at the train wheels," Tessa said. "I didn't think there would be any harm."

"Put that coat on," his mother ordered. "You'll catch your death."

"He was racing the train, and got heated in this warm sunshine," Tessa said. "You know how boys are. I'll carry it for him."

"Please step it up," Mr. Patton said impatiently. "Pole has the car ready, and I need to get down to the office. Wesley, you may leave your coat off if you're too warm."

"You have snow on the back of your new coat," Lucie said as she followed Tessa out the front door.

"Do I really? That silly Wesley was throwing snowballs. He's a great shot. Brush me off will you, Lucie?"

Mrs. Patton shook her head. Wesley glanced up at Tessa and smiled.

CHLOE SEEMED TO BE cooking for extra guests nearly every evening. Tessa was fascinated by the enormous kitchen and the myriad of foodstuffs Chloe had to work with. Wesley and Lucie, she learned, were usually fed in the children's room, while the adults ate in the main dining room.

Jasper had been helping with the cleaning all day, so he was in the kitchen when Tessa arrived to fetch her supper that evening. But Tessa had something other than food on her mind. She showed Wesley's torn coat to Chloe.

"I can stitch the tear," Tessa told her. "I know how to make blind stitches. But I have no button. Do you have any suggestions? I'd like to fix it and get it back in his closet before Mrs. Patton finds it missing."

Chloe was arranging delicate orange slices around a golden roast leg of lamb. "To tell the truth, Honey, that boy got so many coats, it probably never be missed."

"Oh but..."

"I know. Fixing it gonna make you feel better, right? My brother owns a tailor shop over in Greenwood. He gots all kinds of buttons. He surely have the right match. We'll cut off another button and Jasper here can take it and match it up. He'll have another button here tomorrow."

Tessa looked over at Jasper. His bright eyes were shining as he nodded. "Won't take me a minute. I'd be glad to help."

"But I have no money, Chloe. I can't pay for it."

The black woman chuckled as she grabbed another fat orange. "For a teeny weeny little old button? Shucks, my brother don't care about that. He be glad to give away one little old button. Don't you worry none. It's as good as done."

"Thank you both." Tessa fingered the soft towel that was draped over her supper tray. "Chloe, you're a Christian aren't you?"

"I loves the Lord with all my heart."

"I do too. I mean, I do now. Pastor Stedman taught me how to let Jesus to be Lord of my life—all the time. But this afternoon, I lied for Wesley."

"Your conscience bothering you?" Chloe finished the platter and lifted it into the warming oven. She pulled out a crockery bowl bulging with bread dough, and began punching it down.

Tessa nodded. "Wesley put himself in a dangerous place. He jumped on the train as it was pulling out. I sort of rescued him. That's how the sleeve ripped. But then I covered up for him. I lied."

Chloe pulled off a bit of dough formed it into a perfect ball and popped it into a baking pan. "That boy be lonely. The missus don't let him play outside like he need to. He need to be sledding down that hill out there, and racing around the block with the other boys. But she don't let him."

"I sensed that."

"So he do silly things to get attention. It's a shame you have to lie for him, but he don't need no more trouble from his Mama."

"He smiled at me."

"That's good. That's real good. Maybe he got a friend in you now. God be big enough to forgive you for lying child. Soon as you ask him to." She looked up from her roll-making. "Just so's you don't get in a habit of it."

"My conscience hurts so bad now, I don't see how I could make a habit of it."

Chloe gave another deep chuckle. "That's good. That's real good."

Tessa picked up her tray to go. Chloe finished with the rolls and opened the door to the black iron oven and placed the pan inside. Pushing her hair from her face, she said. "Say child, what you gonna wear to this here party you going to?"

Tessa stopped in her tracks. She thought a moment. "I have a church dress. It's going to be at the church."

"But it's a party. You got a party dress?"

Tessa shook her head.

"My niece used to be about your size. She's a little plumper now that she been married a while." Chloe patted her own ample middle and laughed. "But she gots a little blue dress, decked out with white ruffles. I know she don't mind lending it."

"Oh, Chloe, I couldn't."

"Why not? Because we's black?"

Tessa walked back toward her new friend. "Never that, Chloe. Color makes no difference to me. It's just that..."

"Then it's settled. I'll bring that little dress over in the morning when I come. And what about your hair? You gonna do it different?"

Tessa thought about what Erik had said about her hair style. She steadied the tray in one hand and touched her braids. "I could never cut my hair."

"Nobody said nothing about cuttin'. Jasper, did you hear me say cuttin'?"

"No ma'am."

"See there? How about you curl it? Like that little fairy tale, about Rapunzel. 'Let down your hair.'" She gave another jolly laugh. It made Tessa laugh just to hear it.

"But I've never done that. I don't know how." Her hair had been safely tucked away in braids for as long as she could remember.

"My sister-in-law runs a beauty shop over in Greenwood. I could bring one of her curling irons. I show you how to use it. It'd be easy on your nice straight hair. It's not that easy with this." She touched her black curls.

"Maybe I'm more like Cinderella than Rapunzel. Thank you, Chloe. You're so kind."

Chloe waved her hand. "Ain't nothing. You'll just have a whole lot more fun if you feel good about how you look."

Tessa turned again toward the door. "Thanks again. I'll talk to you in the morning."

As she went out the door, Chloe called after her, "And that young man who's friend to your cousin—he gonna love that little blue dress with your blue eyes. Whoo-ee."

Tessa felt her face flush hot as she quickly closed the door. But she hoped Chloe was right.

Chapter 9

At nearly eight Friday evening, Tessa stood before the mirror in her bedroom. The blue dress was a perfect fit. Tessa fluffed the frothy white organza ruffle at the neck. She'd never worn a dress with such a sweeping neckline. Three rows of ruffles around the wrist of each sleeve matched the one at the neck.

Chloe had showed her how to fasten her hair at the nape of her neck and curl the long ends. She even curled the tendrils that usually hung straight about her face. How different she looked.

Tessa took her new coat from the wardrobe and pulled it on, careful to lift the curls out of the collar. Then she arranged them to lay over her shoulders. The temperature had plummeted, so she had no choice but to wear the muffler over her head. She had no smart fur hat like Sadella's. Last of all she pulled on her warm mittens.

As she stepped out of the stairwell of her apartment and into the icy air, she heard the unmistakable rumble of a Model T. Headlights appeared at the front gate. Following the paths that Jasper had shoveled, she made her way, fighting down her nervousness as she went.

The car was filled with laughing, chattering young people about her age. Erik stepped out of the rider's side and gave her a hug in greeting. "Welcome, little cousin. I'm so glad I found you in that department store!"

After helping Tessa into the front seat, Erik crawled into the back, and introduced her around. With a pang of disappointment she saw that Gaven was not among them. Driving the motor car was a young man named Walter, and hanging tightly onto Walter's arm was a curly-haired girl named Verna. In the back seat were two more girls,

Pauline and Iris. Pauline was a plain-looking large-boned girl, while Iris was more slender and wiry. They appeared to be close friends.

Everyone was in a jovial mood and Tessa was met by a bevy of friendly greetings. The giggles and silly remarks coming from the back made it obvious the girls were excited to have Erik in their midst.

"Was your cousin the last one on our list to pick up?" Walter asked Erik as he backed the car out of the drive.

"This is it," Erik answered. "On to the church."

"You're working for the Pattons?" Verna asked. She turned toward Tessa, but never let go of Walter's arm.

"Yes, I just started."

"Isn't it a bit scary? The family seems so aloof."

"Somewhat, I guess."

"Tessa's the tutor for the two younger children," Erik said. "She's already been teaching for a year and a half at a country school near the Glenn Pool." There was a note of pride in his voice.

Verna seemed impressed. She smiled. "You're a teacher? Gosh, all I do is operate an elevator all day."

"I'm sure you do your job well," Tessa offered.

"Well, I meet scads of interesting people."

Tessa wondered if Gaven would be at the church. After all, he was the one who encouraged Erik to invite her. She watched the street signs as they turned onto Boulder Avenue. A few blocks up Boulder and there before them loomed a massive stone church with every window lit up. She craned her neck to look up at the impressive bell tower.

Walter pulled into a parking lot which was already filled with other automobiles. Tessa felt another flutter of nervousness. This church was a great deal larger than Pastor Stedman's little country congregation.

Erik jumped out quickly and assisted Tessa. "I'll introduce you around little cousin. No need for you to feel out of place."

She followed the group up the stone steps into the wide wooden front doors. Pauline and Iris were still twittering and giggling, and Verna was still attached to Walter.

"They're engaged," Erik whispered to her as the couple preceded them down a narrow hallway. Turning a sharp corner, they came to the stairs that led to the basement. Sounds of laughter and music filtered up to meet them, mingled with aromas of cider and popcorn.

Erik led her to the cloakroom and was helping off with her coat, when someone said, "Here, I'd like to do that."

Tessa turned to see the bright smile and gentle eyes of Gaven MacIntyre. He was dressed in a thick cowl-neck sweater, and pleated trousers. The soft cream color of the sweater accented his ruddy face and dark hair.

"Be my guest, pal," Erik said, stepping back.

"I'm so pleased you could make it," Gaven said as he took her muffler and coat. "I wanted to come along to fetch you, but I was helping set up. I'm the co-chairman of all the goings on here."

"I guess I'll leave you in the competent hands of our illustrious co-chairman," Erik said to Tessa as he turned to go. Taking a second glance he said, "Hey, no braids! Good for you. Curls look keen on you."

Tessa's face went hot as Gaven noticed, too. "You look grand. And I like the dress." He stepped back to take a look. "Different than the other day in Vandever's. But even then you were turning heads."

She wanted to protest, but gave a polite "Thank you" instead.

Gaven offered his arm. "Before duties pull me away, let me at least show you to the refreshment table."

Hesitantly she took hold of his arm as he led her from the cloak room. The basement was filled with milling people, who were talking and laughing. The area was divided into three large rooms. The larger room held the refreshment table and Tessa could see a kitchen area behind it with a pass-through window. The two smaller rooms off to the side were filled with children. Festoons of brightly colored paper chains hung about the room.

"This is where we hold Sunday School each week," Gaven explained. "We use those rolling dividers to separate classrooms." He pointed to the wooden devices stacked against a far wall. "We simply push them out of the way for social events."

Tessa wished she had something enlightening to say in response. But she could think of nothing.

"The children worked for hours on the paper chains," he continued. "Many of them helped me decorate."

A few adults had organized a sack race for the younger children at one end of the room. There were cheers of encouragement as the race got underway. Another group played blind man's bluff.

As they neared the refreshment table, Tessa withdrew her hand from his arm. She wasn't sure she'd turned any heads in the department store as Gaven suggested, but she certainly felt the stares as they walked across the room.

"We've planned plenty of games for the little ones; we'll involve the adults later on." Gaven filled a bowl with fluffy popcorn and handed it to her. And elderly lady behind the table smiled as she handed them mugs of steaming cider.

"So you're a teacher," he said as he directed her toward a chair set against the wall. "Isn't that a coincidence that we should be in the same profession?"

"Yes, but it's not the same. I mean, I don't have a degree or anything." Tessa wasn't sure how she could eat popcorn and hold a mug of cider at the same time. She felt incredibly awkward.

"Now what does that mean? I think what you do is extremely challenging. Teaching all levels in one classroom—I'm impressed." Gaven placed his mug on the floor by his feet and then ate his popcorn, so Tessa did the same. "I don't see how you did it when you're so..." Gaven dug at his shirt collar beneath the sweater. "There I go again, referring to your small stature. I'm sorry. In fact, I've not properly apologized for insulting you the night of the storm."

"I didn't take offense," she told him. "In fact, I wish I'd known you were a friend of Erik's. But I'd already had an unfortunate incident with a young man. I couldn't risk another."

Gaven straightened. "What young man? Did someone try to hurt you?"

"It was nothing, really. Only my pride was hurt."

"Then I apologize for myself, and that young man as well."

Tessa smiled at his sincerity. Gaven's dark hair shone like the coat of a chestnut thoroughbred. It was loose and full, not slicked back. "I accept both those apologies, Mr. MacIntyre."

"Hey, I'm plain old Gaven to you. I mean, if that's all right." She blushed and nodded. "So why *did* you quit teaching at the country school and come to the big city? You told Erik it was a long story. I'd like to hear that story."

Thankfully she didn't have to answer him, for at that moment, Iris rushed over to them. "Gaven, they need you at the Victrola. Miss Horner says our music is from the devil. She's throwing a fit."

Gaven turned back to Tessa. When he smiled there was a little line is his left cheek. Not quite a dimple, but almost. "Excuse me a moment. I chose the music myself and I don't think the devil helped me." He wasn't making the remark to Iris, but right to Tessa as his soft brown eyes studied her face. "I'll be right back—I do want to hear that story."

The moment he was gone, she felt conspicuous and awkward, as though she didn't belong here. There was nothing to do but sit. Erik had disappeared as well. She nibbled at her popcorn and watched everyone having a good time around her.

When her popcorn bowl was nearly empty, she saw Pauline step into the room from the outer hall, and glance about as though she were looking for someone. When she spied Tessa, she strode across the room toward her. "I was looking for you," she said. "Didn't you say you're a teacher?"

"I am."

Pauline sat down in the chair that had been vacated by Gaven. "Then you know how to work with children. We need someone to help in another room down the hall. I can't seem to find a volunteer."

"Volunteer for what?"

"A few boys want to have a marble tournament. I need you to supervise." Pauline was standing as though it were settled.

Tessa searched the room for Gaven, and saw him disappearing into the kitchen. He had plenty to do without entertaining her. And besides, this would create a good excuse for her to avoid answering his questions. She smiled at Pauline. "I love marbles. Show me the way."

Following the large girl down the hall, she saw that the basement was larger than it formerly appeared. Pauline took her to a room where seven boys had gathered to set up their tournament. White cloth bags of marbles sat about on the floor. A circle had been drawn in chalk on the hardwood floor, and no one seemed to mind. She had done the same thing on winter days at Independence when the boys became restless and needed an outlet for their energies.

"Boys," Pauline said, "this is Miss Jurgen. She's new in Tulsa, but she's a school teacher and I've asked her to be the supervisor of the tournament." As she named them, they glanced up and gave polite "hellos." "I'll leave you to your task," Pauline said as she went out the door. "And thanks."

A boy named Andrew, who seemed to be the spokesman for the group, stood to his feet and came over to her. He was tall and muscular for his age. "I think we should play for keeps, but Maurice here doesn't think so."

"Let's hear what Maurice has to say," Tessa suggested.

Maurice, a smaller boy looked at her through round eyeglasses. "This doesn't even seem like a real tournament," he said. "We're only having a New Year's Eve party. Playing for keeps is for outdoors. In the springtime."

"I can see Maurice's point. What do the rest of you say?"

The five remaining boys were ready to follow Andrew's leadership, so it was settled. The game was for keeps, and it was for blood. Andrew had a favorite shooter that was the terror of the game. Little by little he whittled down the opponents, but Maurice hung in there. The whooping of the boys as they watched, indicated they were for Andrew. But Tessa could sense Andrew was somewhat of a bully.

None of the other five were playing as hard to win as Maurice. She assumed they didn't want to counter Andrew, but Maurice didn't seem to care. He played with abandon.

"You ain't gonna win," Andrew said after Maurice knocked two of Andrew's favorites clean out of the ring. "Cause I don't lose to nigger lovers."

Maurice's eyes grew large behind his glasses. "Don't call me that. Just because your uncle's in the Klan and hates all the colored people don't mean you can call me names. The Klan's nothing but lawless vigilantes. My dad says so."

Tessa had seen many a rough and tumble fist fight between boys over lesser matters. If she were back at Independence, she'd take them outdoors and let them square off, with her as the referee. But now...

"Yeah," Andrew said as he drew a bead on the next play. "And your dad's always taking up for them colored people like he was one of them. Nigger lover! Nigger lover!"

In a flash Maurice was on his feet, diving into the middle of Andrew. Marbles flew and the boys hollered. Tessa pushed into the center of them as hard as she could to force them apart. "This is the house of God, boys. You'll not fight it out in here. Now stop, or I'll throw you out into the snow."

She was pummeled with a couple of wild jabs, but she held her own, and soon felt them backing off.

"Tell us, Miss Jurgen," Maurice demanded, not taking his eyes from Andrew's face. "Do you think it's right to rule by fear like the Klan does?"

Tessa thought of the incidents Pastor Stedman had read to her from the paper about lynchings, using hot tar and feathers, dragging people behind cars. Whether the victims were white or black, she felt it was all wrong. "No I don't, Maurice. I don't think it's right at all." She heard the other boys gasp.

"But my uncle says," Andrew put in, "that when the law don't do the job right, then citizens have to step in and take over."

Tessa turned to the taller boy. "You know your Bible, Andrew?"

"Some of it I do."

"Never forget it was mob violence that crucified Jesus. They thought they were doing right when they demanded the life of our Lord. Justice is never served by a mob."

Just then, Pauline looked in the door. "Is everything all right? I thought I heard a fight."

"Only a little scuffle," Tessa told her. "But everything's fine now."

"It's time to go back into the main room for singing. Only another hour until nineteen twenty-one!" Pauline looked around at the scattered marbles. "By the way, who won?"

"I judge the tournament to be a tie between Andrew and Maurice. Each is an excellent player."

"I'll tell Gaven. They'll both get a prize. Come on now boys. Pick up the marbles and let's go."

"I just want my taw back," Maurice said to Andrew as he leaned over to grab the big shooter. "You can have the rest." But his bag was still bulging. "And thank you Miss Jurgen for your wise words." He looked back at Andrew. "Some scoundrels need it."

Tessa reached out for Maurice's arm as he went for the door. "Be careful, Maurice," she whispered. "There's a right way to be right and a wrong way to be right. Pride goeth before a fall." But he pulled away and went quickly down the hall.

Mothers had put many of the smaller children down to sleep on the blankets on the cloakroom floor. The children who were not yet sleeping were cranky and out of sorts. The games had ended, and the church was quieter. People were standing about in tight little knots talking. The clinking of dishes and silverware sounded from the kitchen where the ladies were cleaning up. Chairs has been set up around the piano, with a black hymnal placed on each chair. A thin lady with graying hair piled high on her head sat at the piano playing softly.

Tessa wasn't sure what she should do. Gaven was with Erik and a few other men over by the door. However, when Gaven caught sight of her he smiled and motioned for her to come.

"There you are," he said stepping toward her. "I thought you were lost. But I just learned from Iris that Pauline dragged you away to the marble tournament. I apologize. I didn't mean for that to happen."

"Don't apologize. I enjoyed it."

"I appreciate your help. Did you get enough to eat?"

She glanced at the table. There was still plenty of food out. "Actually, I'm still a bit hungry."

"I thought so—after being shanghaied into the nether regions for the entire evening."

Suddenly, loud voices from out in the hall commanded the attention of everyone in the room.

"What in the world?" Gaven spouted. "Another distraction. I'll be right back." He moved quickly toward the door, but not before three men had entered on unsteady legs. Erik was instantly by Gaven's side.

The newcomers looked to be as young as Gaven or perhaps younger. They were dressed in luxurious fur coats. "Happy New Year," the one in the center whooped. The two others merely laughed the empty raucous laughter of drunken men. Tessa had heard it all too often.

"You're in the wrong place aren't you, Harland," Gaven said to him. "This is a church."

"Hey, it's my old buddy Gaven MacIntyre. Ah and good old newspaperman, Erik Torsten. I'm so glad to see my old friends." He reached out for Erik's hand, grabbed it and pumped.

Erik yanked away. "What's the matter, Harland, aren't the parties downtown wild enough for you tonight? Need to come to church for excitement."

"Don't talk to me like that Torsten. I can go anywhere I please. Me and my friends made a bet that we could check out every party in town. Maybe even a few of them colored ones." On this note, his drinking buddies heartily laughed at his lame joke, slapping him on the back. "And you know me—Shelby Harland does not like to lose a bet."

"You've checked us out," Gaven said sternly. "Now leave."

"We haven't checked out everything just yet," he said looking slowly around the room. The crowd was gathering and inching toward the scene of action.

Tessa stood glued to the spot where Gaven had left her.

The man named Shelby Harland spied her and his eyes lit up. "For instance," he said, pushing Gaven aside. "This little number right here. Hello Blue Eyes. Have we met?" He turned back to Gaven and laughed. "You holding out on me boys? Keeping little cuties like this hidden away in church?"

Tessa stepped back as he approached. How she wished she had a board like she used on Jack.

"Who are you Baby Doll, and when did you come to Tulsa?"

Completely unnoticed, young Andrew slipped up between her and this stranger. "Her name's Miss Tessa Jurgen," he fairly shouted. "She lives at the Patton mansion and she says the Klan is just like the people in the Bible who killed Jesus." He looked back at Tessa with a look of defiance.

Whispers rustled through the crowd like wind through a cottonwood. Tessa shivered. She needed the board for Mr. Harland, but a long willow switch would do fine for the likes of young Andrew.

Chapter 10

Shelby Harland took another staggering step, weaved a bit and caught his balance. "My, my. What big ideas for such a tiny little lady."

Before he could finish, Gaven, Erik, and several other men were ushering Mr. Harland and his friends out of the room and down the hall. Gaven went only as far as the door, then turned back to the group. "So why's everyone standing around? Grab a hymnbook. Miss Horner let's start with 'The Old Rugged Cross.'" In a matter of moments, Gaven was by the piano leading the singing, and everyone's attention was diverted. His voice was a strong melodic baritone.

Tessa wasn't sure if Gaven did that just for her, but she was certainly thankful. What a hateful child that Andrew was. Why would he do such a thing? Following the others, Tessa quietly made her way to a chair and turned to the correct page in the hymnal. This was one of Pastor Stedman's favorite hymns. Before the second verse, the words on the page became a blur as tears formed in her eyes. Feelings of homesickness washed over her in deep waves. How she wished she'd never had to leave the Glenn Pool.

At midnight the children who were still awake blew whistles and shook noisemakers. The adults threw paper streamers, and shouted, "Happy New Year." Walter even took the opportunity to kiss Verna in front of everyone.

Tessa was somewhat relieved that Gaven had to remain at the church to help clean up. He didn't even come to say good-by to her, but that was all right too. Who knows what he thought of her after that humiliating scene.

Erik was at her arm as they headed back to Walter's jalopy. The group was a great deal quieter now than when they arrived. When they pulled up to the mansion gate, Erik stepped out with her. In a low voice he said, "I know you probably didn't mean anything by what you said to the boys about the Klan. But you'll want to be very careful what you say in Tulsa. The Klan is powerful here, and word carries like a brush fire in August." He gave her arm a squeeze. "This isn't like where you're from. Just be careful, Tessa. Please?"

She nodded, pushing down the need to defend herself. Deep inside, she didn't feel she had said anything wrong. "Thank you for inviting me, Erik. I had a good time."

"Will we see you Sunday morning? Sunday School starts at nine. Walter and Verna could stop for you."

She supposed she had to go to church somewhere. Even though she deplored the bigness of the Boulder Avenue Church, it was as good as any for now. "Yes, that'll be fine, thank you."

Erik seemed pleased, but she wasn't sure she ever wanted to see Gaven again. She wished she never had to face any of them again. Once inside her door, she realized she never did get back to the food table. But she was too exhausted to care.

AS TESSA OUTLINED LESSON plans in her apartment on Saturday, soft winter sunshine shone all day. By the time she was ready to go to Sunday School on Sunday morning, there were glistening puddles everywhere from the melting snow. She tried to step around them as she walked out to Walter's car.

Tessa had returned the blue party dress and the curling iron to Chloe, so her hair was again in braids atop her head. Dressed in her navy print church dress, she felt more like herself. She carried the black leather Bible that Edith had given her for her nineteenth birthday.

Verna and Walter were alone this time, and were quite friendly. "You can come to my class if you'd like," Verna said as they backed out onto Galveston Street. "I go to the women's Bible study group."

"Yeah," Walter said, "they may try to separate us for Sunday School, but we're together again in church."

Tessa couldn't help but laugh. Silently she wondered what it would be like to care for a man so much she would want to be with him every moment. "Have you set a date for your wedding?"

"Probably around Decoration Day in May." Verna gave Walter's arm a loving pat. "That will be just after Walter graduates from Kendall College."

"Soon to be changed to Tulsa University," Walter added with a note of pride. "Your friend, Gaven, was one of my classmates. He graduated last spring."

Tessa had no idea why he referred to Gaven as her friend, but she let it drop. Gaven's leadership position in the large church, along with being a college graduate, clearly meant he had plenty of young women seeking his company.

When they reached the church, she was unnerved to see Gaven waiting at the top of the front steps in the foyer. His soft tweed suit was in impeccable good taste, the dark shoes polished to a high sheen. Only the stubborn locks of his dark hair would not be tamed.

"There you are," he said, almost out of breath.

She was perplexed as to why he would be waiting for her. She looked behind her to be sure he was truly speaking to her. Verna whisked close by her and whispered. "I'll wait at the end of the upper hall to take you to class with me." She gave Tessa a silly sidelong grin, and hurried on to catch up with Walter.

Gaven came down the steps to meet her halfway. She caught the pleasing aroma of men's cologne. Much nicer than anything Pastor Stedman wore. Her insides felt light and funny.

"Can I talk to you a minute? I haven't much time. I'm assistant to the Sunday School Superintendent and we have a shortage of teachers in the primaries."

Ah so that was it. He needed a teacher. "Of course we can talk, Mr. MacIntyre."

A twinkle in his eye broke through his intense manner. "First names, remember? Here," he directed as he took her arm, "the church office will do for the moment." He guided her into a room banked by high bookshelves, with a wooden secretarial desk situated off to the side.

If he had closed the door, Tessa would have made a break for it, but he did not. "I'm so sorry about not saying good-bye to you New Year's Eve," he said. "I nearly clobbered Erik, for taking you out of there without telling me. I was helping with the cleanup and the next thing I knew you were gone."

He paused, but she could only gaze at him wordlessly. Finally she managed to tell him that Verna was waiting for her down the hall.

"Verna's not going anywhere. And besides, I can show you to the class. There's something else I want to tell you. You now have another chance to ride in that little red roadster."

A magnificent beaming smile spread across his face, and again he seemed to be looking for her response. When she was still quiet, he continued. "Remember the red car I was driving last week when you were out there in the storm?"

She nodded.

"It belongs to our boarding house friend named Mike. I should say, it *belonged* to him. He keeps losing money at the gambling tables at the Hotel Tulsa, and he's agreed to sell the car to me for a fraction of what it's worth. Plus he'll take payments. Isn't that great?"

"I'm pleased for you."

"Will you go for a ride with me next Saturday, Tessa?"

Tessa reached out to place her hand on the nearby desk to steady herself. Mixed feelings surged through her.

"Oh, not alone," he added quickly. "We'll have Verna and Walter with us, or maybe Erik and someone he decides to ask."

It was quiet again. He seemed such a gentleman. If Erik were there, surely she'd be safe. "Thank you," she managed to say. "I think I'd like to ride in that little roadster."

He took a quick breath and moved as though he were going to reach for her hand, but stopped. "It rides nice, and it has a heater too."

She smiled, remembering the warmth of the Willys-Knight. "I'd better go now." She didn't want people to start talking. He stepped with her into the hall.

"Do you still need help in the primaries?" she asked.

He stopped short and looked down at her, eyes sparkling. Now she noticed there was a cleft in his chin, and his jaw had a nice smooth line to it. "I sure do," he said. "Are you willing?"

"Actually, that's the very place I'd be the most comfortable."

"We'll tell Verna, then I'll take you downstairs." When he offered her arm, she shook her head and he dropped it. But as they walked down the hall, she could feel his sleeve brush against her coat, and an odd warm feeling rushed all through her.

Church service in the imposing and solemn sanctuary was nothing like being in the small country church with Pastor Stedman at the pulpit. Tessa wondered how anyone could know about salvation by hearing such a weak sermon as was given that morning. As she studied the people about her, she was surprised that few carried Bibles to follow the scripture readings. They seemed detached rather than involved in the preaching.

After church, Gaven was waiting for her in the same spot where he'd been standing when she arrived. "May I walk you to the car?" he asked politely. She allowed him to guide her through the crowd to the parking lot beside the stone building. "I'll call for you at one-thirty

Saturday afternoon," he told her as he held the door for her and closed it after her.

The image of his gentle smile burned into her mind as Walter drove back toward the mansion. "My, my," Verna said with a chuckle, "you've been to this church only twice and already you've raised more eyebrows than most people do in a lifetime."

Tessa wasn't sure if the comment was an accusation or a compliment. "I haven't done it intentionally."

"I know." Verna turned to her and smiled. "I think that's why it seems so refreshing."

ON MONDAY MORNING, Tessa let herself be duped into thinking that her relationship with Wesley would be changed, due to the incident at the Frisco Station. But she was sorely mistaken.

She arrived early in the children's room in order to be fully prepared. Since she'd been in the room last, someone had brought in a teacher's desk and a wooden swivel chair. That was a relief, as she'd wondered how she would present a sense of decorum without a desk at which to be seated.

After studying the room, she pushed the children's desks away from the book shelves over to the windows. She turned her desk to have the windows at her left, and turned the children's desks to face her. Perfect.

The door opened. Mrs. Patton ushered a sullen Wesley, and bright-eyed Lucie into the room. Kipsee followed on their heels.

"Good morning Miss Jurgen. I'm pleased to see you are prompt." Her cool gaze critically appraised the new arrangement of the desks, but she said nothing. "Children," she instructed, "this will not be a play time. Stay in your seats as long as school is in session. You are to obey Miss Jurgen at all times. Is that understood?"

Lucie hurried to the desk nearest to Tessa before Mrs. Patton finished with her speech. Wesley dragged along behind.

"Yes, Mother," Lucie called out. She was dressed in a pale pink dress with ribbons and ruffles. Her long dark ringlets lay over her shoulder, stark against the pastel.

"Wesley?" Mrs. Patton's soft Southern drawl tightened. "Do you understand me?"

"Yes'm," he grumbled.

The door closed quietly. Kipsee moved to a corner to lie down as though he knew it wasn't time to play.

"May Sophia sit at my desk with me?" Lucie wanted to know.

"Sophia would be a distraction at your desk," Tessa explained as she went to retrieve the doll from the cherry wood doll bed. "But let's have her sit in the window seat where she can see how well you do in your lessons."

Lucie clapped her hands. "Oh, I like that idea."

Wesley slouched at his desk and refused to look up. Perhaps she should have left him to his fate on the train last week. Surely she'd made a mistake to side with him.

"Wesley, you will begin in the McGuffey's Fifth." She placed the open book before him. "Since we've recently had a heavy snowfall, please read the poem 'It Snows.'"

With head down, and words mumbled, Wesley began:

> *"'It snows!' cries the schoolboy, 'Hurrah!' and his shout*
> *Is ringing through parlor and hall,*
> *While swift as the wing of a swallow, he's out*
> *And his playmates have answered his call...'"*

Wesley paused and looked out the window. "I don't get to go out much when it snows. No playmates answer my call."

"If it snows again, I'll request permission for us to build a snowman," Tessa told him.

Wesley looked at her momentarily, but looked away again. "Permission won't be given."

"Let's not make hasty conclusions," she said. "Please finish the poem."

By the time the morning was half over, Tessa could see Wesley had no intention of obeying either his mother or her. While Lucie was reading, he went to the play area and brought two toy airplanes back to his desk. She made him return them, but while he was to be writing arithmetic problems, his paper was filled up with drawings of airplanes. He at least read what she asked him to read, but there seemed to be a brick wall when it came to arithmetic.

She asked for Chloe's input that evening, but Chloe had no advice. "I ain't no teacher, Miss Jurgen. And Jasper knows more about arithmetic than I does. He's gonna be the first one in our family to graduate. But that little Wesley, why he's just plain old lonely."

Tessa thought about her comment. Why did Wesley's parents refuse to let him have friends over? Suddenly she was hit with a thought. "Chloe, does Wesley like Jasper?"

Chloe stopped sifting with the sifter in midair. "Like Jasper?" Her eyes were wide. "What you talking about, child?"

"I just thought that a fine young man like Jasper might be a good influence on Wesley."

"Whoa now. There you go again. Ain't nobody in this house care to have a black boy be no kinda influence on their precious little offspring. Leastwise, they wouldn't think it was a *good* influence." She shook out the rest of the flour and stirred the batter she was mixing. "Face it, girl. You's the only influence Wesley gots at this here moment."

Tessa mulled over the situation as she ate supper in her apartment. Perhaps she could be the playmate Wesley needed. At least some of the time. She pushed her plate to the side of the table, and brought out a sheet of paper. She quickly penned a chart which entailed a series of rewards for work done. The rewards would be games played together on Friday.

WESLEY SEEMED TO SHOW a twinge of interest as he listened to her explain the idea the next day. He was at least ready to work on his memorization and recitation and his list of spelling words. But arithmetic was still a struggle. By Thursday, he had earned almost enough points to have a game of marbles. When they dismissed that afternoon, he was studying the chart, which was posted on the wall near the windows.

"Anyway, I didn't want to play marbles by myself, and Lucie sure can't play."

"I can so," Lucie snapped back. "But I don't want to play Ringer. I have enough points for Chinese checkers."

"I was going to challenge you, Wesley," Tessa said.

He looked surprised. "You?" He savored the thought for a moment. "Naw, you don't even have any marbles, and besides, I don't want to play a girl."

Tessa kept her eyes on her work at the desk. "If you're not afraid of losing your old marbles, you can give me a shooter and a few aggies to start, then we'll see who can play," she said.

He was quiet a moment. "How can I get two more points?"

"You tell me."

She could tell he was studying the chart. "Miss only one word on my spelling test."

"That's right."

"And if I don't make it?"

"You'll study spelling while Lucie has a play time."

On Friday morning, to her surprise, and probably Wesley's as well, he made a one hundred on his spelling test. After lunch, it was playtime.

Lucie's time was first, then Tessa and Wesley squared off at the chalk circle she drew on the hardwood floor.

Wesley generously gave her a few to begin with, along with a nice shooter. It felt heavy and cool in her hand. He seemed to watch with new interest as she got down on all fours to play beside him. She took several of his best aggies before he could gather his wits about him. Soon the three of them were whooping and laughing as the game grew more heated.

Suddenly, the door flew open. There stood a shocked Mrs. Patton. "Miss Jurgen! What in heaven's name are you doing on the floor?"

Chapter 11

Tessa stood to her feet and smoothed the front of her dress. "Wesley earned playtime by gaining points..." she began.

But Mrs. Patton was in no mood to listen. "Please come to my office. We need to see about this. Children, please quietly read until Miss Jurgen returns."

"Yes, ma'am," Wesley answered.

"But Mother, Miss Jurgen..." Lucie attempted a defense, but Mrs. Patton shushed her with a raised hand. "I'll hear it from Miss Jurgen thank you."

Tessa followed Mrs. Patton's large figure down the hallway to her office, which was on the far side of her husband's. Mrs. Patton seated herself at a small roll top desk and waved Tessa to a delicate chair with a pink brocade cushion. From this room, Mrs. Patton almost single-handedly ran the social life of the city—or so Erik said.

"Miss Jurgen," she began, "there is absolutely no reason for you to be on the floor playing with my children as though you were some type of ragamuffin. I expect you to handle yourself with the highest degree of decorum. What do you have to say?"

"You're absolutely right, Mrs. Patton," she replied, and could see she put her employer off guard. "I should never have yielded to the temptation to become a playmate to Wesley and Lucie. I let my feelings for their loneliness momentarily outweighed my wisdom."

"Whatever are you talking about? Loneliness. Our children are not lonely."

"In one way they aren't. They have a room full of toys and books. And they have each another. But in another way—in the lack of friends their own age they're very lonely." Tessa scooted toward the edge of her chair. "When the weather warms up, I'd like to ask your permission to take the children around the neighborhood. Especially late in the afternoon, so they can play with other kids after school."

Mrs. Patton's hands were clasped solemnly in her lap. "The neighborhood is full of riffraff. We must be careful."

"Among the riffraff, I'm sure there are many good, well behaved children. I'd be there to keep watch."

She was quiet a moment. "I suppose it might be permissible. I'll talk to Mr. Patton this evening to learn his feelings."

Good. Tessa was hopeful that Mr. Patton would agree with her. "And meanwhile, I'd like permission to show Wesley the rudiments of playing Ringer so he'll be prepared when he goes out to be with the other boys."

"Ringer?"

"Marbles."

"On the floor?"

"I know of no other way, ma'am. They roll off a table."

Mrs. Patton loosed her clasped hands and toyed with the strand of rope beads at her bosom. The ring on her finger glinted with a blue light. "I'll ask his father," she said.

"Thank you. May I go now?"

Mrs. Patton waved her away. As Tessa approached the door, she stopped a moment. "By the way, Wesley made a one-hundred on his spelling words this morning." Mrs. Patton merely nodded.

Back in the children's room, Wesley and Lucie greeted her with questions in their eyes. "For the time being," she explained, "I'm not to play on the floor with you."

"Shucks," Wesley said.

"But your mother will be asking Mr. Patton tonight for permission for me to teach you further. That is, if you want to play against me."

Wesley laughed in spite of himself as he surveyed the interrupted game. "I'm glad we weren't playing for keeps. How'd you learn so good?"

"My brother, Berg, taught me. He was the best. We won all the marbles that were to be had at our little country school."

"Does Berg still play marbles?" Lucie wanted to know.

Tessa was seated at the teacher's desk, and Lucie came close to snuggle. "Berg is in heaven, Lucie. He died of pneumonia two years ago."

"Ooh." She looked up at Tessa, her dark eyes wide. "That's so sad." She glanced at her brother who was on the floor trying again to aim his shooter for a straight shot. "Even if Wesley is mean, I wouldn't want him to die."

Wesley looked up. "I am not mean."

"Sometimes, you're mean," Lucie insisted.

"Well," he said rolling the shooter around in his hand. "I don't intend to be."

Tessa took a deep breath. Perhaps they were making progress.

"Miss Jurgen, last spring when I was playing up the street the boys got mad because my steelie chipped a boy's glassie. They said I was cheating."

Tessa moved her swivel chair away from the desk, closer to the chalk circle, then pulled Lucie onto her lap. "A steelie is unfair, Wesley; it's too heavy. Most tournaments won't allow them to be used at all."

Wesley shrugged. "How was I supposed to know? Nobody told me. A big kid named Andrew called me a baby for using my knuckle pad, so I threw it away. I thought he was going to beat me up when I shot with the steelie."

Could this be the same Andrew whom Tessa met on New Year's Eve? There was a similarity. "The more you practice, the tougher your knuckles will become. You won't need a knuckle pad."

"Will you help me?"

Rather than leaving at her usual three in the afternoon, Tessa stayed until four, coaching Wesley in how to aim and shoot straight. When she arrived at her apartment, there was her first pay envelope tucked in the mailbox inside the stairwell. She opened it and felt the bills crisp and solid in her hands.

There was also a letter from Pastor Stedman. Inside was a note from Mama as well. She hurried upstairs to read it. Pastor indicated that Papa knew she was gone, but still had no idea where she was. Neither Pastor nor Mama mentioned whether Papa was angry, but she had no trouble reading between the lines. It suddenly occurred to Tessa that Papa could become violent and force Pastor or one of the board members to tell where she was. If he came after her... She pushed the frightening thought out of her mind.

Mama's note was full of love. She proclaimed her joy and pride in Tessa. The girls couldn't quite understand where their sister was, nor why she wouldn't be coming home on the weekends. They had each signed their love in pencil at the bottom of Mama's note. Tessa ran her finger over Siegrid's neat penmanship, and Vega's awkward scrawl. The homesickness was a heavy weight inside her. And back of it all was the constant gnawing fear that Papa might do something awful. When he was full of moonshine whiskey, he was no longer Papa, but a wild man.

SATURDAY MORNING TESSA walked to Elgin Street in the brilliant sunshine, and rode the trolley to the market to purchase groceries. But first, she went to Kress's and bought a curling iron. Before Gaven came to call, she wanted her hair curled. And she wasn't sure just why. It was the first time in her life she'd ever purchased a frivolous item for herself.

Later, putting each grocery item away in her own kitchen gave her a feeling of accomplishment like nothing she'd ever known. Pastor and Edith had shipped the remainder of her belongings and now the apartment truly felt like home.

Gaven was due to pick her up at two. The closer it grew to the time, the stronger the giddy excitement grew inside her. Rather than honking at the gate, Gaven startled her by knocking at the door to her stairway. She quickly pulled on her coat and flew down the stairs. She opened the door to see his warm smile widen in approval of what he saw.

"Ah, curls again. Nice." He took her arm as he closed the door behind her. "Very nice." The sunny afternoon allowed him to be coatless. His brightly colored sweater vest was pulled over a shirt, open at the neck. Guiding her toward the car, he said, "Your red chariot awaits."

She was hopelessly tongue-tied when he spoke to her, but he seemed not to notice or care. Walter and Verna were snuggled into a corner of the back seat. Tessa had hoped it would be Erik who came along. She could see Walter and Verna weren't going to amount to much as chaperons.

"What would you like to see?" he asked when they were seated inside the snappy little roadster.

She wasn't sure since she'd seen so little of the city.

"How about the campus? I'd like you to see my alma mater."

He turned around to Walter. "Shall we drive out to Kendall?"

"Sure, why not? I only see it every day of the week," Walter answered with a twinge of sarcasm.

"Maybe you do, but Tessa's never seen it."

So it was settled. The roadster was warm inside just as Gaven had promised. Tessa watched with interest as they drove through town and then east toward the college. Gaven pointed out a few of the buildings on the way. Watching him as he talked, Tessa tried to imagine him dressed in his uniform marching down the streets of Tulsa in the celebration parade following the war. Someday she would ask him about the war. But not now. Now she wanted only to think about good, happy things.

He and Walter told about pranks they had pulled as lower classmen beginning at Kendall. It made her wish she had been there—been a part of the gaiety of college life.

Kendall Hall was a fortress-looking, three-story building with a massive bell tower at the top. To one side was Robinson Hall, with Kemp Lodge on the other.

"I'd like to show you the library," Gaven said after parking the car and helping her out. "That is, if you want to see it."

"I want very much to see it."

"I thought so." To Walter, he said, "Are you coming, Walt?"

"Give the little lady the grand tour. Verna and I will be here when you get back."

As Tessa walked up the stairs into the arched entryway with Gaven, she tried to imagine what it would be like to walk these halls as a student. Suddenly she realized she wanted very much to be able to attend college. To earn her degree.

"Are there many women students here?" she asked quietly.

"Quite a few. Why?"

"Just wondering." She walked on, but Gaven stopped and tugged at her sleeve.

"Wondering about what?"

She shook her head. "Nothing." Papa had always scoffed at her desire to study and learn. "Book-learning ain't for women," he told her. But she noticed it wasn't for him either. He seldom read anything. Not even a newspaper.

Gaven seemed to accept her reluctance to open up. They stepped into the library with its impressive rows of bookshelves. Being Saturday, the room was quiet. A young librarian sat at the wooden desk by the windows. Several students browsed the stacks; others sat at the desks studying.

The thought of so many books in one place was unbearably exciting to Tessa. She longed to run her fingers along the backs of the books; to touch each one. Oh to be able to have the leisure to sit by the windows at the study desks and read. What a warm contented joy that would be.

"Your blue eyes are shining," he whispered. "Do you like this place?"

She nodded. "Very much." If only she could tell him how much. When she was in school she often hid her books, and tried not to let Papa catch her studying too much. And never let him catch her reading just for fun. Berg was good about pretending they were his books borrowed from the small school library, and not hers.

After showing her a few of the classrooms and a chemistry laboratory, Gaven took her over to Kemp Lodge. They strolled across the wide veranda-type porch and into the stone building where he showed her the chapel and the cafeteria. The chapel was especially serene and peaceful. As they walked back to the roadster, she was quiet.

"Many of the women students I know are working to pay their way through school," Gaven told her.

How had he known what she was thinking?

"Others," he went on, "have academic scholarships. Very few are actually wealthy. In fact, most of the high-dollar oilmen like the Pattons and the Harlands send their kids back east to school. Not to Kendall."

She smiled. "I know. They're afraid of the riffraff. Whatever that is."

"Riffraff is anything they're not."

"It doesn't make much sense—being that rigid. Especially with their children."

"I agree. And speaking of children, how's the tutoring work coming?"

Tessa marveled at his ease of drawing her into conversation. He seemed to know just what to say to help her through the awkwardness.

As they drove back toward Tulsa, she explained about the difficulty in getting Wesley to study and work. And how her plan to play a game of marbles with him got her in trouble. As she described Mrs. Patton's anger, Gaven threw back his head and let loose with a clear full laugh.

"How I would have loved to have seen that. I bet you gave him a lively game."

"It wasn't too funny for me," she assured him.

"No, I'm sure it wasn't." He struggled to contain the laughter. "What's Wesley interested in? Have you learned that much about him?"

"Airplanes."

"Ah. I might have guessed. Most boys are. I happen to have a couple of books on airplanes in my classroom. I could loan them to you for a time. You could use them as supplemental reading. As an incentive—along with the marbles, of course."

Tessa could imagine how excited that would make Wesley. "Oh, would you?"

Gaven looked over at her. "To see your eyes light up like that? I sure would."

She felt the warmth flooding to her face, and Walter chuckled from the back seat.

As Gaven drove down main street to go to the Riverview School, he pointed out the building that housed the *Tulsa World*. "Your industrious cousin is working right in there today," Gaven told her. "It seems there's another black guy in jail and things are getting heated up in town."

"What did he do?" she asked.

"You mean Erik?"

"No, the black man in jail."

"No telling," came Walter's reply from the back seat. "Those niggers will do most anything. I hear tell they're building an arsenal in one of those churches over there in Greenwood. If they're not stopped, someday the whole blamed bunch will be in an armed revolt."

Tessa felt a small shock wave move through her. She thought of Chloe and Jasper and Pole and knew that couldn't be true of them. Who was Walter talking about? She waited for Gaven to refute this terrible comment, but he was silent. Did that mean he agreed? Surely not.

At the school, Gaven ran inside to get the books from his classroom. "I hope these help," he told her when he came back out and placed the books in her lap.

She ran her hands over the well-kept books with brightly colored covers. "He'll be delighted.

"Where to now?" Verna wanted to know.

"Standpipe hill," Walter suggested, and Verna giggled. "A great way for Tessa to see the city."

"It is at that," Gaven agreed and headed the red roadster north from town up a rolling hill to a pasture-like area which overlooked the entire skyline of Tulsa. There they parked, and in the late afternoon sunshine, the straight rows of tall buildings of the thriving city glowed before them.

Verna and Walter decided to get out and take a walk.

"You'll freeze," Gaven told them. "The sun will be down in a little while."

"Don't worry, pal," Walter quipped. "We know how to keep warm."

Tessa looked away, astonished at his audacity.

"Don't mind him," Gaven said. "He's just a little crazy in love."

Gazing at the scene before her, Tessa changed the subject by asking about different landmarks in the city. Presently, she asked, "Where's the town of Greenwood that I've heard so much about?"

Gaven gave a little laugh. "Greenwood's not a town. It's a street."

"Are there two Greenwoods then? The place I've heard about is a town where businesses are located." She remembered what Chloe said about the tailor and the hairdresser.

"You're talking about the colored section of town. The whole area is called Greenwood because of the street." He pointed off to the east. "It's over in that area north of Archer. Most all those houses off in that direction are in the colored section. Churches and stores too."

"And schools?"

"And schools."

"Why?"

"Why what?"

"Why are they separate?"

"It's best that way, Tessa. The blacks belong with their own people. They're better off there."

Something unexplainable bristled deep inside her. "How can a person be better off being separated from other humans? How can they be better off by having to sit in the back seats of the trolley? Or to stand if there are no seats left?" Tessa had seen this for herself that very morning. She was appalled.

"Tessa, you're still new in the city. Later, you'll understand. That's just the way things are. It can't be changed." He reached to touch her arm, but she pulled back.

"Then how does that make us any different than the Pattons? Doesn't that make the blacks a type of riffraff to us? Didn't Jesus die for them the same as for us?"

At that moment, Verna and Walter came shivering and giggling back to the car. Verna's bright red lipstick was smeared. With the couple intertwined in the back seat, Gaven drove back to the Patton mansion in silence.

Chapter 12

G aven parked at the gate and walked her to the door of her apartment, then surprised her by asking to pick her up for church the next morning.

"That is, if you don't mind going early," he said.

"I don't mind."

"Eight-thirty too early?

"Eight-thirty is fine. I'll be ready."

He touched the brim of his hat. "Thank you for going along this afternoon. I enjoyed it a great deal."

"Thank you for inviting me. The tour was perfect." She lifted the books she was carrying. "And this is a grand idea. I'm sure Wesley will rise to the bait."

He nodded and started to turn, then as an afterthought said, "Maybe we could take young Wesley out to the airport sometime. That is, if his mother would allow it."

"That's a fine idea." She wanted to comment that perhaps Mrs. Patton would consider the two of them to be riffraff, but she thought better of it. Perhaps it was best to let the matter drop. "I'll ask and see."

He touched his hat again and was gone.

Later in her apartment she puzzled over the comments Gaven had made about black people. How could he be a leader in his church and still think as he did? She wished Pastor Stedman were here so she could ask him about it.

But still and yet, he'd asked to call for her again. And in spite of their confrontation, the thought of being with him again sent currents of warmth radiating all through her. There was a quiet strength about Gaven that endeared him to her.

As she hung up her coat, she remembered how he had sensed what she was thinking about attending Kendall College. Closing the wardrobe, she picked up the airplane books and sat in the rocker in the corner of the bedroom. He had cared enough to explain the possibility of scholarships as though he knew she was concerned about lack of finances. Such sensitivity from a man was bewildering to her.

She riffled through the books and studied the pictures. Some of them looked like Wesley's toy planes. Gaven had even been sensitive to her problems with Wesley. She was anxious to try the books as an incentive, and anxious to see if Mrs. Patton would allow them to take Wesley to the airport.

BY THE END OF JANUARY, Tessa was feeling almost smug about her work with Wesley and Lucie. Their father had given permission for her to continue to coach Wesley in playing Ringer. He had also agreed that under her supervision, and when the weather warmed up, they could take outings in the afternoons. She felt she should wait to ask about taking Wesley to the airport. No sense in pushing too much too soon.

Wesley continued to flounder, however, with his multiplication tables. One day, early in February just before six weeks tests, she hit upon an ingenious idea. She would teach multiplication to Wesley using the marbles to explain number sets. He was thrilled as he caught onto the concept of two sets of nine glassies, or three sets of six aggies.

"This makes sense," he exclaimed. He saw that it also applied to his collection of airplanes. And later, he thought of using a deck of playing cards.

"Multiplication is simply a quick way of adding," Tessa told him. "We use sets of numbers rather than single numbers." Wesley seemed to want to know the *why* behind everything. He took nothing at face value. Now that he had caught the concept, Tessa was sure he would have the tables memorized before spring.

But her euphoric feelings were dampened one morning when Lucie and Wesley arrived in the room with dour expressions. "Both of you are close to earning playtime on Friday," she said, "so why the long faces?"

"It's Sadella," Wesley said plopping down at his desk.

Lucie avoided her desk altogether, choosing rather to crawl up in Tessa's lap. "She's coming home next Monday."

"But why?" Tessa asked. "The semester's barely begun."

Wesley's chin was propped in his hand. "She got into trouble and they kicked her out."

"Oh no."

"She didn't want to go anyway," Lucie put in.

"Yeah," Wesley agreed, "and I bet she got kicked out on purpose."

Tessa tried to think what it would be like to have the angry Sadella back in their midst. "What did she do to get kicked out?"

"Who knows? Nobody tells us anything," Wesley said. "But I bet it was something wild."

"But she's your sister. Surely you're happy that she's coming home."

"She's mean," Lucie said snuggling into Tessa's shoulder. "You said the other day that Wesley was mean," Tessa reminded her.

"Sadie's lots meaner than Wesley." Her little voice lifted in emphasis.

"Lots meaner," Wesley agreed.

"All right," Tessa said, trying to shake off the premonition she was feeling. "We can't sit about moaning." She gave Lucie another little squeeze and set her down. "We have work to do. Let's pull our minds back to our lessons." Lucie slowly made her way to her desk and sat down. "This week your points may earn a Friday afternoon outing."

This brought a ray of light to both faces. "Keen!" Wesley said.

"That is, if it stays warm." She looked out at the sunshine.

Immediately Wesley studied the chart to see how close he was. Tessa could tell he was determined to make it. As the day progressed, she tried not to think about Sadella. What difference could it possibly make to her? Her work was with Wesley and Lucie.

TESSA WAS THANKFUL on Friday afternoon that both Wesley and the weather cooperated. The day was splendid.

Lucie carefully placed Sophia in the pram with the wrought iron handle and spoke wheels, and covered her with doll blankets. She was determined to push the pram on their walk. Tessa wasn't sure, but decided to let Lucie learn for herself.

Together the three of them strolled down the street lined with majestic homes. She studied the deep wrap-around porches of the impressive stone and brick structures. One particular house with a rounded pillared entry way was especially fetching. Wesley informed her it was the Harland home.

"Where Shelby Harland lives?"

"Yeah," he said as he swung his chamois bag bulging with marbles. "And all the rest of his family. Shelby goes to college back east somewhere."

"Is he there now?"

Wesley shrugged. "I dunno. Probably."

She looked again at the picturesque house and wondered about the drunken young man she'd seen New Year's Eve.

Lucie surprised her by keeping up. Each street was not only paved, but had nice concrete sidewalks. In each yard, plantings of small trees looked like fat sticks in the ground. Tessa could imagine them in a few weeks as each one budded out with tiny pale green leaves.

In a vacant lot near Riverview School, stood a giant solitary cottonwood. Tessa brought along a quilt, and they had talked Chloe out of a few freshly-baked sugar cookies, which were wrapped in a small towel in the pram beneath Sophia. Lucie suggested they spread the blanket beneath the cottonwood and eat their cookies.

"But there's no shade from the tree," Wesley countered.

"We'll pretend there are leaves and that it's spring," Lucie said, and Tessa was in full agreement. Her heart longed for spring, even though she wouldn't be in her beloved hills where the dogwood would explode into soft pastel bouquets.

As they crossed from the sidewalk to the tree, it was more difficult for Lucie to push the pram over rough dried grass, but she never complained. Nor did she ask for help. Tessa marveled at the girl's even disposition. They spread out the quilt and had eaten most of the cookies when they noticed groups of children filtering out of the school building.

Wesley's eyes lit up. "I'd like to play at least one game, if I may," he said lifting his marble bag.

Tessa knew he'd been waiting for this. "Do you think they'll be playing? It's still so cold." In spite of the bright sunshine, there was a chill in the air.

"All I can do is find out."

"Where?"

"They play beside the school—on the school grounds."

She gazed over at the long low modern brick school building. Gaven would be working in his classroom there. Probably getting ready to go home. "You may go, but only one game."

He nodded and she felt that at last they had come to an understanding.

"Try not to get dirty," she called after him.

A few minutes later, as she and Lucie were deep in a conversation about why grass turns brown in winter, Gaven's red roadster came driving by. She was sure he wouldn't notice them sitting there, but he noticed. He parked the car, stepped out and called a friendly hello.

He looked tall and lean against the pale winter sky as he strode purposefully toward them. Gaven always appeared to know who he was and what he was about. There was so little hesitation in him. Even his walk was determined.

"A little early for a picnic isn't it," he said as he came near.

"We're pretending it's spring," Lucie announced clearly. She was another one who knew what she was about.

"What a great idea," Gaven said, speaking directly to Lucie just as a teacher would. "So you're also pretending that you're warm, am I right?"

"My coat is warm, and Sophia is covered up."

Indeed, Lucie's coat was heavy and the matching bonnet and muff were keeping her well protected.

Gaven gave a chuckle at this remark. "And how about you?" he asked Tessa.

"My pretender isn't quite as high as Lucie's but I'm faring well, thank you."

"May I join you?" He waved at the blanket.

"We're out of cookies," Lucie told him bluntly.

Gaven laughed again, the laughter sounding warm and friendly on the cool clear air. Tessa liked the sound of it. "Please sit down," she told him. "And pretend the ground is warm."

"I know who you are," Lucie said to Gaven.

Gaven pushed his hat back. "Oh you do?"

She nodded as she busied herself taking Sophia from the pram and fussing with the bow on the lacy bonnet.

"So who am I?"

"You're the man who comes calling for Miss Jurgen. Chloe says you're Miss Jurgen's beau."

Tessa's cheeks grew hot. She had no idea she was being watched; nor that Lucie would be so talkative. "Lucie, really. You're not supposed to tell everything you hear."

"I don't tell everything. Just the most important thing."

Now both Gaven and Tessa laughed and his eyes locked with hers as they shared the joke.

"I know who you are, too," Gaven told Lucie. "So there."

Now Lucie looked up. "You don't know me."

"Sure I do. You're Lucie Patton. And somewhere around here there is a brother named Wesley."

Lucie looked at Tessa. "Gosh, he really does know."

"See, I know important things too," he said, and now Lucie laughed.

"Wesley's playing marbles with the boys." Lucie pointed toward the school.

The roar of a car engine suddenly drowned out their conversation. A silver Kissel speedster came racing across the grass right toward them and slammed to a stop within a few feet of the tree. Gaven was instantly on his feet. Out of the car stepped Shelby Harland.

"Well, well, MacIntyre. Look at this cozy little country picnic. Am I interrupting anything?"

"My daddy doesn't like him," Lucie said in a loud whisper to Tessa.

"Aw, what does he know, you little peanut," Shelby said.

"Look Harland, no one invited you here. And there's no need for you to be rude to a little child."

"And this is the young lady who had her gorgeous golden hair all in long curls at the New Year's Eve party." Shelby circled around Gaven to come nearer to Tessa. "I bet you thought I wouldn't remember."

"I never gave you another thought at all," Tessa told him.

"Well, I can't say it's been mutual. I've thought about you a great deal."

Gaven took a step toward Shelby. "I thought you'd be back in school by now, Harland. Aren't you missing out?"

"Aw, my old man told me to sit out a semester. He wants me to think about where I'm going." He leaned nearer to Tessa and in a flash yanked her muffler from her head.

"Give that back!" she demanded jumping to her feet.

"Oh heck," he said. "Braids. Where are those beautiful curls?"

"Give the lady her scarf," Gaven told him sternly.

"Oh dear," Shelby said in a mocking tone as he waved the bright muffler, "I'm shivering with fright. Whatever will I do?" But he was backing away from Gaven as he spoke.

"It's all right, Gaven. Let him take it. I don't mind." It was her only muffler, but she didn't want them to come to blows over it. Already her ears were getting cold.

"See what a sweet little lady she is, MacIntyre? She wants me to have it. As a little memento of how much she likes me."

"I doubt that," Gaven said.

Shelby flared at that remark. He stopped his backward retreat. "You don't know anything. I'm as good as you are any day. Now if you'll get out of my way, I'll return the scarf myself. I don't need you telling me what to do."

Tessa was mortified at the whole scene. Why did this man have to intrude into her life? Gaven gave in and moved out of the way as Shelby came back to Tessa with the muffler. He knelt down on the blanket and placed it on her head and gently draped the long-tasseled ends over each shoulder. His young eyes were looking at her, boring through her.

"You have the most beautiful clear blue eyes I've ever seen," he said softly. "Like the most lovely blue sky in springtime."

"You gave her back the scarf, Harland, now get your hands off her."

Tessa was certain Gaven was going get in a punch, but just in time, Shelby leaped to his feet and danced backward toward his car. He opened the door and started to get in. He pointed to Tessa giving his most handsome smile. "I'll see *you* later."

Chapter 13

Soon after Shelby drove away, a proud Wesley came running across the lot from the school. "I lost," he yelled to them sporting a big grin and waving the bag. "But not by much. And they can see I'm a good player now." He skidded to a halt near the blanket, barely giving Gaven a glance. "I'll be a real threat by the time the spring tournaments come, Miss Jurgen. That Andrew is nothing but a little scaredy cat."

"Wesley, I'd like you to meet Gaven MacIntyre. This is the man who loaned us the airplane books."

Tessa was impressed that Wesley used his manners and shook hands and thanked Gaven and even said how much he like the books.

Gaven wanted to load the three of them in his car and take them safely home, but Tessa refused. "I have permission to take them walking. I have no permission to take them in a motor car with someone who's a stranger to their parents."

"I'll park on the street close to the house then, and watch to see that he doesn't bother you again."

"Who bother who?" Wesley wanted to know.

"Mean old Shelby Harland," Lucie told him. "He was trying to flirt with Miss Jurgen."

Wesley wrinkled up his nose. "Gee, you didn't let him did you, Miss Jurgen?"

His innocent remark seemed to break the awkward tension and Gaven's laughter filled the air.

"I tried not to," she told him. "Now let's get home. This has been adventure enough for one day."

True to his word, Gaven was parked part way between the Harland and Patton mansions. Shelby was nowhere in sight. As the trio walked by the roadster, Gaven smiled and doffed his hat. Lucie sang out, "Thank you Mr. MacIntyre." As they turned in at the gate, Tessa heard him drive away.

IT WAS A SOBER BUT smug Sadella who stepped off the train on Monday. This time, there was no ruckus from Wesley. On the contrary, he stayed close by Tessa's side. She wondered why she and the younger children had been required to come. It was terribly uncomfortable. The ride home was in silence. As Pole dutifully unloaded the baggage at the house, Mr. Patton ordered Sadella to meet him in his office.

Wesley glanced up at Tessa and raised his eyebrows. Within a week, however, Sadella was happily driving her own sleek black coupe to Tulsa High School each day. Whatever had happened at boarding school was evidently quickly forgotten. Tessa marveled that there was no evidence of discipline for Sadella's wrongdoing at school.

ON VALENTINE'S DAY, Gaven surprised Tessa with a lovely floral-and-lace card expressing his fondness for her. He took her out to dinner at the restaurant of the Hotel Tulsa. She knew it was far beyond his budget, but it was a glorious evening. Slowly, she was learning to talk to him without freezing up. Her trust in him was growing. Seldom did Walter and Verna join them; no chaperon seemed to be needed.

Tessa found when the spring flowers arrived, that she barely thought of the dogwoods in the hills back home. In Tulsa, there were flowers at every hand. Hardly was there a yard that was not full of brilliant yellow forsythia bushes, nodding jonquils, and rainbows of iris and tulips. In the exhilarating spring sunshine, she and the children took walks two and three times a week. Was it springtime, or was it Gaven making her heart sing?

One Saturday, she and Gaven were given permission to take Wesley to the airport. He was in awe watching the open cockpit planes taking off and landing. The pilot flew low, tipped the wing, and waved to them. It made Tessa's heart jump just to watch them. Such daring.

"Someday I'll be up there flying," Wesley told them as he shaded his eyes against the bright afternoon sun. "I'll be a pilot and have my very own airplane."

"You can do anything you set your mind to do," Gaven said, as he gave the boy a reassuring pat on the shoulder. "Don't be afraid to dream big."

LATE IN MARCH, MR. and Mrs. Patton made preparations to leave for New York City for a short stay. Tessa met with them in Mr. Patton's office as they explained what was expected of her in their absence. She would conduct school each day as usual, and also eat supper with the children, staying with them until they went to sleep. That meant she could not go to the mid-week Bible study with Gaven. Nor could they go for their usual ride together on Saturday afternoon.

"Wesley has a dentist appointment downtown on Tuesday," Mrs. Patton was saying. "Leave Lucie with Chloe and take the trolley. Wesley will want to stop at the five and dime and buy something. Allow him to do that."

Tessa nodded as she scribbled notes. The conversation seemed to be coming to a close and nothing had been said about Sadella. At length, she asked, "Is Sadella going to New York?"

The two parents exchanged glances. "We wanted her to," Mr. Patton said, "but she doesn't want to miss classes. Since she's just beginning, we feel that's best."

Still they were not addressing the issue. Tessa pressed them further. "Please tell me—am I responsible for Sadella while you're gone?"

Mr. Patton cleared his throat. "No. We hired you as nanny for Lucie and Wesley, not Sadella. Sadella is old enough to take care of herself."

"Thank you, sir."

Tessa asked for a few more clarifications before she was dismissed.

When she took the children for a walk early the next week, she was surprised to see Sadella's coupe parked at the Harland mansion.

"Sadella likes Shelby," Lucie said with a twinge of disgust.

Wesley shook his head. "I wonder why?"

But Tessa saw it clearly. Shelby was a bright, exciting, handsome older man to Sadella. He would hold much allure for one so young.

As instructed, Lucie stayed with Chloe on Tuesday afternoon, and Tessa and Wesley caught the trolley at Elgin and rode downtown. The day was windy, gray and drizzling, so Tessa brought along Mr. Patton's large back umbrella.

Wesley was terrified of going to the dentist. Tessa had been to a dentist only once in her life, and it wasn't too nice an experience. If she were his age, she too would be frightened.

"Let's ask the Lord to help you," she suggested.

His eyes grew wide. "Would He do that? God's pretty busy with other important things, isn't He?"

"The Bible says He knows the number of hairs in your head. That's how important you are to Him. He cares about everything that concerns you."

He thought about this a moment. "I never knew that."

She took his hand, and there on the trolley, she said a short prayer for God to be with him and to calm his fears.

A happy boy emerged from the dentist's office into the waiting room. He plopped down beside her and announced in a whisper, "He did it."

After having read two ladies' magazines, Tessa nearly forgot what he was referring to. "Who did what?" she asked.

Wesley pointed toward heaven. "He helped me."

She squeezed his hand and smiled. "God's so faithful."

At Kress's Tessa wasn't surprised when Wesley wanted to look at marbles. "I don't have any cat eyes," he said. He chose a package of ten and studied them closely. Pointing at a pack of fifty he said, "I have enough money to buy these, but it doesn't seem fair. The other boys can't buy that many."

Tessa was proud of his thinking and told him so. They bought a few pieces of penny candy for fun, and tucked two pieces away to give to Lucie later.

As they came out of Kress's, the drizzle had turned to sprinkles, but the two of them fit nicely under the big umbrella. As they headed back toward the trolley, Tessa heard a voice calling her name. Her first thought was of Gaven. Turning around she saw Shelby running toward them.

"Hello, gorgeous." He pulled his hat down against the rain drops. "Going home?"

"We're taking the trolley."

"My car's right up the street. Come on, I'll take you."

"No thank you," Tessa told him.

"You don't need to play games with me, Tessa. MacIntyre's not here now." He grew serious, just as he had the day he put the muffler around her. "Look I'll not behave ungentlemanly." He put up his hand. "Really, I'd like to be able to help you. It could start pouring any minute."

The sound of a blaring horn sounded from the street. It was Sadella in her coupe speeding down Main Street. The little car was loaded with laughing students. She waved and called out in a shrill voice, "Hello Shel."

Shelby looked her way briefly and gave a half-hearted wave. "How about it, Tessa?"

"Thank you for your concern. Wesley and I will be fine." She put her hand on Wesley's shoulder and turned to go.

"If Mr. MacIntyre were here, you would ride with him."

"You bet we would," Wesley piped up. "He loaned me two books on airplanes and he's nice."

"Shh, Wesley." She squeezed his shoulder. "That's not true, Mr. Harland. If Gaven were here I would still refuse. I was told to use the trolley to take Wesley to the dentist and I'm following the instructions."

"Well then," he said walking alongside as they headed in the direction of the trolley line. "Would you go with me this Saturday night? To dinner?"

"I must be with the children this week."

"Next week then?"

They crossed the street at the intersection and Shelby was still right beside them. Sadella's coupe flew past them again splashing water everywhere. She again called out to "Shel." This time he ignored her. "How about it?" he asked again.

Tessa stopped short. "Please stop annoying me, Mr. Harland. I must get Wesley home."

Now he was in front of her. "A nice dinner. Just you and me. At the Hotel Tulsa. Have you ever eaten there?"

She thought of the special time she'd spent with Gaven at the hotel on Valentine's Day. "No thank you," she said firmly. They pushed past him. Shelby was soaked, but he didn't seem to care. One more time he asked, and one more time, she refused. As they boarded the trolley, he could be seen running back to where his car was parked.

When they stepped off the trolley near Fourteenth Street, the rain was coming down in bucket loads. "Come on Wesley, you've always wanted to walk in the puddles. Now you have no excuse not to."

"Whoopee," he shouted and jumped purposely into the first one he saw.

There in front of them was Shelby Harland in his shiny silver car. Tessa could hardly believe her eyes. But before she could get near, Sadella drove up, her coupe now empty of all the boisterous riders. "Get in you two. You look like a couple of drowned rats."

"Come on, Wesley." Tessa gave him a little shove. Even though it happened to be Sadella, she was thankful to be rescued from one more confrontation.

"Aw, I was having fun," Wesley said.

"No argument." She nodded toward Shelby's car, and Wesley immediately got the message.

At the house, Sadella stopped under the portico to let them out. Wesley hopped out and ran toward the house. Tessa turned to Sadella. "Thank you so much."

The girl looked at Tessa with fire in her eyes. "I only stopped to keep you away from Shel. He liked me for a long time before *you* came along."

"I've done nothing to encourage his advances, I assure you."

"What difference does that make?"

The girl was impossible to argue with. It was useless. "Thanks again for the ride." Tessa opened the door and stepped out.

"Somehow, someway, I'll get Shel back."

"I certainly hope you do." She closed the car door with a firm slam.

Chapter 14

On Friday night, Sadella had several friends in. They gathered in the vast ballroom in the north wing and cranked up the Victrola, which sent ragtime and fox trot music reverberating through the house. Tessa heard the shouts and laughter, and was thankful when Wesley and Lucie finally went to sleep so she could retreat to her apartment. She was also thankful she'd not been given the responsibility to keep the rowdy girl corralled.

Chloe was spending each night sleeping in a room near the children. Before leaving the house, Tessa stopped by the kitchen to see her friend, and was surprised to see her arranging a cut-glass platter of crackers and cheese.

"Are they making you work this late?" Tessa asked.

Chloe looked up and rolled her eyes. "Land sakes, I ain't sure what's going on. All I know is I gots to do what the little princess wants or I'll catch fire for it later."

"Want me to help?"

Chloe shook her head. "Can't do that. Miss Sadella would love to catch me in some wrongdoing like that. Jasper been helping me. I just sent him on home." She put the finishing touches on the tray. "I told Miss Sadella I'd do one more tray then I gots to be with them little ones."

"I'll see you in the morning then."

But Chloe was hurrying out the other swinging door and didn't answer.

A sharp cold north wind hit Tessa in the face as she stepped outside. She snuggled up her coat and pulled her muffler over her head. The weather seemed to forget that spring had arrived. Shouts from out near the street startled her. Evidently, a few of Sadella's guests had ventured outdoors. Tessa wondered how many of them there were. It was best to ignore them.

As she reached her apartment door, the shouts grew louder. She turned to look and there in the headlights of a Model T was Jasper surrounded by a crowd of white boys. "Hey nigger, what y'all doing out here, huh?" one boy hollered.

"You're in the wrong part of town, black boy," another yelled. Other inaudible taunts followed.

Tessa's heart hammered in her throat. This couldn't be happening. Before she could even think, she was running toward them yelling, "Leave him alone. He works for the Pattons! Leave him alone, I tell you!" She pushed into the center of the circle standing close to Jasper. The rancid stench of liquor hung in the cold air. They were a bunch of drunken kids.

"Which one of you wants to face Mr. Henry Patton when he comes home if you harm this boy? With his money he could press charges against every one of you. And win!" There was silence. She turned to Jasper. "Jasper, you get on home."

"Thank you, Miss Jurgen," he said quietly. The circle opened to let him out. Jasper walked a few steps and then broke into a run.

"Ha," said a tall thin boy, "them niggers sure can hightail it when they're scared."

Tessa stepped nearer to the drunken boy. "All of you get out of here before I call the police."

"The police wouldn't care," said a voice behind her. Tessa turned to see long-legged Sadella standing there in the cold wind, dressed in a short, flimsy red dress with row upon row of fringe dangling and shining in the headlights. A slender cigarette dangled in her fingers. "The police don't like niggers any more than we do. Right boys?"

The group mumbled their agreement, but nothing like the shouts of a few minutes earlier.

"She ordered us to go home, Sadella," said the tall boy.

Sadella sauntered closer to Tessa and glared down at her. "How dare you order my guests away? This is my home, not yours."

"If you allow these drunks to accost your employees, then you're not taking very good care of *your* home." Tessa turned and walked quickly back to her apartment.

"Nigger lover!" Sadella shouted after her. "You know what we do to nigger lovers in Tulsa?"

Tessa closed her apartment door on the stinging words.

A FEW DAYS LATER, WHEN Mr. and Mrs. Patton returned, they questioned her closely as to what went on in their absence. But since they'd given her no authority, she felt no responsibility to tell them anything. They should have either taken Sadella with them, or left a responsible adult in charge. Their weakness at handling their own daughter was repulsive to Tessa.

When she tried to tell Gaven about the incident with Jasper, he was strangely noncommittal except to warn her to be very careful. "It doesn't take much to rile up the Klan," he said.

She wanted to press the matter, but she remained silent. Because of all his wonderful qualities, it was easy to push the matter aside. It wasn't worth causing a disturbance. She couldn't remember ever being as happy as she was when she was by his side.

At Pauline's request, Tessa had become a member of the Literary Guild at the church, and then was elected secretary of the group. She found the readings and book reviews stimulating and thought provoking. She now had her own library card and to Tessa's sheer delight, she had time to read in the evenings.

One evening she met Pauline at the Carnegie Library where they spent time discussing upcoming programs for the guild. Tessa had come to appreciate Pauline's straightforward, no-nonsense personality. The two were growing to be good friends. They were paging through a volume of Carl Sandburg's poems when they heard a commotion by the windows.

"I wonder what's going on?" Pauline said as she put down the book.

Others were now moving from the bookshelves and tables toward the windows to look out. People were talking in hushed tones. Tessa saw one woman cover her mouth as though to stifle a gasp. She grabbed Pauline. "Let's look."

Rather than going to the crowded windows, they stepped out the front door onto the sidewalk. There before them was the most ghastly, terrifying, sight Tessa had ever seen. White-hooded, white-robed people, hundreds and hundreds of them were marching down the Tulsa streets. There was no march music, no shouts of gaiety. In fact, there was barely any noise at all. Only the eerie sounds of the feet tramping down the street.

Tessa looked at the shoes. Men's shoes, women's shoes, and even the shoes of little children. How could there be women and children among them? Some carried torches, in spite of the fact that it was barely dusk and the street lights were coming on. Smoke and sparks from the torches curled and flickered upward.

All along the street, people stood watching. Curtains and blinds rustled and moved in the windows as more citizens came to view this strange sight.

Tessa stood transfixed. So, these were the people who committed all the unspeakable acts she'd heard and read about. But here they were brazenly walking down the street. Tessa wondered why the good citizens of the community didn't run them out of town. Perhaps Gaven had been right about not stirring up their wrath.

"I've lived here all my life," Pauline said in a soft whisper, "and I've never seen anything like this."

"I hope I never see it again," Tessa said as she turned to go back in the library. Pauline followed her, but all interest in poetry was suddenly gone. "How can they do the things they do and get away with it?" Tessa asked.

Pauline shook her head. "They think they're doing right."

"You don't agree with them, do you?"

"Good heavens no. But what does it matter? You saw how many there were, and I bet that's not all of them. I've heard there are thousands of them across the state."

That night, Tessa tossed and turned in her bed, as nightmares of white robes, flaming torches, knotted hanging ropes, and screaming black folks haunted her.

The next day, a formal invitation arrived in the mail from Gaven inviting her to go with him to the Spring Fling at the church on Saturday night. Pauline had described it as their "social event of the year." This good news helped overpower her memories of the Klan march.

With invitation in hand, she hurried to her wardrobe to see about what to wear. Three new dresses now hung there, and the pink one would be perfect for the party. Chloe had taught her how to shop in the bargain basements of the downtown department stores. She felt a twinge of pride at her wise purchases. Thankfully, Mrs. Patton had never said another thing about shopping for her.

The white linen collar of the pink dress sported a touch of ruffled lace, with a bow at the front. She pulled the dress out and arranged the fussy sash at the waist, then stood back to look. It would do fine. On the floor of the wardrobe sat her new dress shoes which closed with a strap across the top rather than lacing up. She'd worn them to church once, now she could wear them to the party as well.

The late March wind was gusty the night of the party, but the frigid chill had disappeared. As she stepped from her apartment hooked on Gaven's arm, the clouds above them appeared to be whipped around through the stars by the winds. She was surprised to find Erik and a new girl in the back seat of Gaven's roadster. Gaven had told her he never knew who Erik was going to be with from day to day. Evidently there'd been several girls in his life, but he wasn't ready to settle down with any.

She was politely introduced to the girl whose name was Dorothy. Dorothy's hair was done in soft waves, with a bang on her forehead, not unlike Sadella's. In Tessa's opinion, she was sitting too close to Erik for their first outing.

From the back seat, Erik said, "Say cousin, I understand from Gaven that you recently took on a gang of hoodlums out on Galveston Street. Aren't you a bit too small for that role?"

Tessa twisted around to look at her handsome blond cousin. "David didn't let his size stop him from slaying Goliath. It doesn't take much to scatter a bunch of bullies."

"What happened?" Dorothy wanted to know. And as if he had been there, Erik proceeded to tell the story.

Tessa corrected a couple of details he had misconstrued, then said, "Small wonder things like that happen among the kids in Tulsa," Tessa said to him, "when even the newspapers encourage acts of violence. Adults in this city set very poor examples."

Erik leaned forward. "Now what's that remark supposed to mean?"

"Don't your read your own paper? Or maybe you help write some of that trite nonsense."

"Tell me what trite nonsense you're referring to and I'll tell you if I wrote it."

"I'm talking about the way the paper encourages mob violence. Just recently an article openly spoke of a possible lynching."

Erik shook his head. "You know I wouldn't write anything like that. You must be talking about the cover story where the headline mentioned getting out the 'hemp.'"

"That's one among many. How can your conscience allow you to stay in such a place? Can't you do anything to stop it?"

"Cut me a little slack, Tessa. I'm just a cub reporter."

"She's a tough one to argue with, Buddy," Gaven put in. "Just as well give up."

Erik shrugged and sunk back into his seat, and Dorothy immediately grabbed hold of his arm.

"And speaking of arguing," Gaven went on, "this is too beautiful a night, and too wonderful an occasion to argue. What say, let's drop it."

His comment made Tessa ashamed she'd brought it up. It *was* a wonderful evening, and Gaven helped to make it so. He was not on any committee for this party, and he was by her side the entire evening. There were games and refreshments. And even a few waltzes, since Mrs. Horner wasn't there to keep guard over them. The chaperons who were there didn't seem to mind at all. The joy in Tessa's heart was close to bursting. She felt secure and safe gliding about the floor in Gaven's strong arms. The lovely music from the Victrola seemed to wrap around them and meld them into a oneness. When Gaven smiled down at her, she felt she could hardly breathe.

When they came out of the church late that evening, the wind had mercifully ceased. The radiant stars were rejoicing at having won the battle against the clouds. The beauty of their diamond brilliance made Tessa want to reach up and pluck one. And she felt almost tall enough to do it.

Later, as Gaven walked her to the apartment from the car, his hand was boldly around her waist and she allowed it to remain there. He stopped at her front step, reached into his pocket, and pulled out a long black hinged box. "I've been wanting to give this to you all evening, Tessa, but there never seemed to be a proper moment. Let this gift always remind you of our perfect night together."

The box was velvety-smooth in her hands. Inside, lying in the pink satin lining was a string of pearls. Never had she ever imagined wearing anything so elegant. So exquisite.

"Allow me." Gaven gently lifted the strand from the box, opened the clasp, and fastened it around her neck. His hand remained there touching her neck, then her cheek. "They were beautiful lying in the box, but even more beautiful on you."

His other arm slipped easily around her, and she felt the warmth of his soft lips closing over hers. For a moment, time ceased being, as she felt herself melt into him. Had he not been holding her, her legs would have crumpled beneath her.

"My little Tessa," he said snuggling her close to his chest. "I care for you so very much."

She cared about him too—more than she had ever thought possible. But her senses were spinning, and her throat closed. Tears burned hot in her eyes. He touched her chin, tilting up her head. "I've made you cry. Have I done something wrong?" He pulled out his handkerchief and dabbed at her cheeks.

"The gift is so sweet." She pulled back and reached up to touch the cool pearls. "I've never received such a fine gift. Thank you, Gaven. Thank you very much."

He touched her lips with one more quick brush-like kiss. "The pleasure is all mine. I'll be here in the morning to take you to church. Good night."

Tessa stood inside the enclosed stairwell for a few moments, leaning against the wall, trying to steady her shaking legs and slow her ragged breathing. What could such a fine young man like Gaven see in a little country girl like her? She was mystified.

Tessa was halfway up the stairs when a soft knocking at the door stopped her.

"Miss Jurgen? Miss Jurgen? It's me, Jasper. Can you open the door?"

Tessa's face flushed as she thought perhaps someone had been watching them. She hurried down to open the door.

"Can you come with me to the house, Miss Jurgen? You suppose to call somebody by the name of Pastor Stedman. Says they's been an emergency."

Tessa's thoughts flew to her mother and sisters, and panic gripped her. "What kind of emergency?"

"Mr. Patton done talk to him. He only says you suppose to call. He says to use the telephone in the downstairs library."

God, help me stay calm, her heart cried out. She followed Jasper across to the house and in the back door. The house was quiet. Pole and Chloe were waiting in the kitchen.

"There you is, child," Chloe said jumping up. "Jasper tell you?"

She nodded mutely.

"This way, Little Missy," Pole said. "I show you to the library." He led her out of the kitchen and down the hall. She'd never been in the downstairs library. She barely noticed the floor-to-ceiling shelves full of enticing books. Pole led her to a desk, and handed her a slip of paper. "Here the note with the number you gots to call."

"But what about the charges?"

Pole's dark eyes softened. "Mr. Patton, he say it be all right. I be waiting right outside."

She didn't recognize the number. Central came on the line and she read the number from the piece of paper. A woman's voice came on the line amidst the crackling static. "May I speak to Pastor Stedman, please?" She fought to steady her voice.

"Tessa. Oh Tessa is that really you? This is Edith."

"Edith what is it? What's happened. Is Mama all right?"

"Your mama and sisters are fine now, Tessa, don't worry about them. It's your father." There was an endless pause as though she were searching for words. "He was shot earlier today."

Chapter 15

A gasp caught in Tessa's throat. Her legs gave out and she collapsed into the chair situated at the desk. "Is he...?"

"They got Doc there as soon as they could, but there wasn't a thing anyone could do."

Papa. Dead. "How...? Who did it?"

"The details aren't clear, but there was an argument. Your father was angry and went gunning for another man. It had to do with a whiskey deal."

Always the whiskey, Tessa thought. And now it's taken his very life.

"The other man was shot in the leg," Edith went on, "so the officials are calling it self-defense."

Tessa was sure it was self-defense, knowing the measure of her father's violent anger. "Where's Mama?"

"She's right here, Tessa. And this is our new phone you're talking on. She wanted us to call and tell you. Here, you can talk to her yourself."

The melodic sound of Mama's Swedish voice came on the line and Tessa was finally able to let loose and weep. They talked in short clipped sentences, saying nothing. Saying everything. Mama said the girls were upstairs in Tessa's old room sound asleep. They have no more fear now, Tessa told herself. No more fear.

"We have a small service on Monday, Tessa. The Pastor is good to officiate."

"I can take the train out on Monday morning."

"No Tessa. Best you stay there. Please. It's better that way. An ugly thing, murder is. Don't come. We keep it small and quiet. The sooner over, the better."

"But I want to be with you."

"No, please. Your life is there now. Be a good girl and stay. Bye now, Tessa. Here's the good Pastor."

At the sound of Pastor's kind gentle voice, Tessa was again reduced to tears. He expressed his sorrow at the tragedy, then he too asked that she not come. "We don't want to draw attention, Tessa. The whole thing is an ugly mess."

"I'm coming, Pastor. I'll see you on Monday," she said firmly. "And thank you for caring for Mama and the girls."

In the kitchen, Pole, Jasper, and Chloe sat and listened as she explained what had happened. Chloe fed her hot corn bread and warm milk.

"Your pastor's right—you sure enough don't want to take that old train," Chloe told her. "All them roughnecks heading for the oil fields to go to work. On a Monday morning, you be the only little lady amongst them. That's no way to travel."

"God will take care of me," Tessa told them. Inwardly, she hoped she was right.

When Gaven came by to pick her up Sunday morning he immediately sensed something was wrong. But when he asked, she told him only briefly that her father had died. She longed to be able to tell him every ugly thing, but there was no reason to burden him. She could hardly grapple with the truth herself.

Following church, Gaven drove her home. "The Glen Pool's not far," he said, as he parked at the back gate of the mansion. "I can get the day off and take you down."

Inwardly she recoiled. She couldn't bear the thought of his knowing. "Don't take off work on my account. Your students need you," she said.

He reached out to take her hand. "I'd count it a privilege to be able to help you.

She shook her head. "I can't let you. But I'm grateful for the offer." Slowly she pulled her hand away. Would he feel the same if he knew what her father was like? Later she'd tell him all the details, once she was able to sort them out in her own mind.

There was hurt in his eyes. She could sense his deep sincerity. "Won't you reconsider? I could call the principal this afternoon..."

He was making it so difficult. "I'd better go in. I have a number of things to take care of this afternoon."

He released a sigh of resignation. "What a strong-minded girl you are. All right, I'll stop insisting. I'll talk to you again when you get home." At her door, he gave her a warm hug, but did not kiss her. She was glad.

Midway through the afternoon, there was a knock at the apartment door. It was Jasper. "Mama says for you to come over," he told her. "She gots to tell you something."

"I'll get my coat."

As they walked back to the house, Jasper said, "I'm beholding to you for helping me the other night when them white boys had me trapped. You're a mighty kind lady."

She smiled up at him. "I'm so glad I was there at the right moment."

"Me too."

Chloe and Pole were together in the kitchen as they had been the night before. "We found a way to take you to the Glenn Pool quick and easy," Chloe told her. Her dark eyes were twinkling. "You tell her, Pole."

"My friend, Lendy, drives a taxi. He say he'll run you down there for the price of a train ticket."

"But taxis are much more expensive than the train," Tessa protested. "I couldn't let your friend do that. All that way. And he'd have to wait. I don't know how long it will take."

Pole stood up. "He already say he'll do it, Miss Jurgen. I done ask him."

Tessa looked at Chloe who was smiling and nodding. "You just get yourself over to the trolley line in the morning right at seven-thirty. He be waiting for you there. No need for nobody here see you getting into a colored man's taxi. I'll tell Mr. Patton where you gone."

As she ran it through her mind, it seemed to be the quickest way to get there and back.

"What you say, child?"

"I'll go. And thank you." She looked around at the three of them. "Thank you so much."

LENDY, WAS A PLUMP, happy young man. He talked a great deal, but not in a wearisome way. The trip out of Tulsa was pleasant in spite of the circumstances. Her trip along this road the week before New Year's seemed so long ago, and she felt years older. The countryside was dressed in the soft green of spring, and occasionally there would be delicate pink and white dogwood in bloom.

Siegrid and Vega were overjoyed to see her. They tumbled about her like two puppies. Both were delighted with Tessa's curled hair and wanted to touch each ringlet. The hugs from Pastor, Edith, and of course, from Mama, filled her full till she felt she would surely burst from feeling so much love. No one mentioned the fact that she'd been instructed not to come.

Lendy planned to wait in the taxi, but Pastor and Edith wouldn't hear of it. He was invited inside to sit at their table and eat the noon meal with them. Tessa smiled as she saw how Siegrid and Vega studied his friendly black face. Tessa prayed that her sisters would never hate because of color.

Kind people from Pastor's church came to express their condolences. Tessa was pleased to talk to those whom she'd been close to. They wanted to know all about her life at the Patton mansion, but she was quick to explain it wasn't as glamorous as it sounded. Later, Tessa walked with Mama over to the church to spend a few minutes before the service.

"What will you do now, Mama?" she asked, as they stepped out into the bright spring sunshine. "You can't stay out there on the place."

They walked up the stone steps and into the quiet of the church. The casket loomed big at the altar of the small sanctuary. Tessa stared at it a moment.

Mama lifted her shawl from her crown of braids and let it lay over her shoulders. "The landlord already has told us we cannot stay. He makes the decision for us." She gave a wry smile. "Pastor has offered to let us stay here for a time." She laid her hand on Tessa's arm. "The money you send, it helps so much. I can't tell you."

"The Lord's blessings, Mama."

"Edith says I can sew for women. That will help a little."

They moved toward the front and sat in a pew together. There was so much Tessa wanted to say, but the sight of the plain casket seemed to silence them both. How confusing to know the one who had made their lives so miserable was now gone. And yet he was the very one who had given Tessa life. She had wanted so desperately to love him, and now her feelings were even more mixed up. Why did everything have to be so complicated?

Soon the little church filled with a handful of parishioners who didn't seem to care that this whiskey dealer had been murdered. Their love extended to the survivors. And Tessa felt the love.

In the service, Pastor explained gently that Aldan Jurgen had within him the capacity for good, just as all of them in the church had that capacity. "He could have lived for the Lord, just as we choose to live for the Lord. But remember, we also have the capacity to commit violent acts—and without Jesus, perhaps some of us would. Let's not judge harshly this man. For we don't know the forces that drove him to live as he did."

Tessa held Mama close. Edith was nearby with the girls on each side of her. Tessa could tell they loved Edith already. That was good. Now Edith would have two new girls to take Tessa's place. One of the ladies played the piano and they all sang "The Old Rugged Cross."

Strong men carried the casket out the church door and over to the cemetery where the grave was dug. The aroma of freshly- turned dirt filled the air. Pastor Stedman said a few words there as well. But later Tessa couldn't remember for the life of her what they were, because suddenly there was Hod Latham. Broad-shouldered and bow-legged, he stood there glaring at her from beneath the broad brim of his greasy hat. The edge of his blanket-lined overall jacket flapped in the wind. Thankfully, most of the people had left.

"Howdy, Tessa." He stepped closer. Tessa could see the veins bulging at his temples. His deep-set eyes, shelved over with thick dark brows, were sullen. "You think just 'cause your old papa got hisself shot that the deal is off? You think you can hightail it to Tulsey and hide away like a little rabbit? You better think again. I aim to make you my woman."

Pastor and two of the men stepped between Hod and Tessa. "You're interrupting a funeral service," Pastor said firmly.

"No I ain't. The service is done finished. I watched." He pointed to the taxi, where Lendy was leaning on the hood. "You getcha a nigger boy in Tulsey, did ya, Tessa? This here your feller?"

Tessa bit her lip to keep silent.

Without taking his eyes from Hod, Pastor said, "Tessa, go on to the house. Gerda, Edith. Go with her."

Mama put her arm around Tessa and drew her toward the house. "I tell you to stay away, now you see why. He comes after you."

"I ain't done with you, little lady," Hod yelled after her.

"Get out of here Latham," Pastor said with a steady voice, "or I'll have my wife call the sheriff."

Hod let out a whoop that chilled Tessa to the bones. "You think I'm feared of that dumb old scalawag? You must be teched in the head." He gave another horse laugh that echoed out across the cemetery. But as Tessa stepped up on the front porch, she saw he was backing away.

"Don't think I won't find you, Tessa," he yelled. "Your papa give you to me fair and square and I mean to settle up soon. I'm getting real impatient."

Tessa wanted to scream at him. Mama pushed her through the front doorway. Edith and the girls were on their heels. Tessa moved quickly to the bay windows. Pastor and the other men were standing firm without moving. Mama was right—she should have stayed away. Her presence placed all these gentle people in danger.

Hod shook his finger at Lendy, who was now inside his taxi. "And you, nigger. You better keep yourself out of my territory if you know what's good for you."

No one spoke. No one answered him. Slowly he kept backing away yelling as he went. Tessa saw through the lace curtains that his old mule was hitched to a tree down the road beyond the church. Papa may be gone, but his unfinished business was very much alive.

Saying good-bye later that afternoon, wrenched Tessa's heart. The visit had been brief and painful. She tried to take a few moments to explain to the girls about her new home and about Wesley and Lucie. But time was so short, and she felt it was best for Lendy to get back before dark.

On the way home, she found herself profusely apologizing to Lendy for the awful scare she put him through. "And after all your kindness to me," she said.

"Now don't you fret none, Miss Tessa," he told her. "It was plenty worth it just to meet that nice old white-haired pastor and his kind wife. They done make me feel like a king."

He was right. Pastor and Edith made everyone feel like royalty. And now her own mother and sisters were basking in that love. Tessa would never cease being grateful to them.

"Seems to me like you're the one should be watchful for that Hod rascal. It ain't none of my business, but what's he talking about you being his woman?"

"Moonshine whiskey was always getting Papa into terrible trouble. A few months ago, he made some insane deal with Hod Latham, and I was the payoff. He's the reason I left there and came to Tulsa."

"Good thing you left, Miss Tessa. Good thing you get away from the likes of that man. But moonshine makes many a man seem more than they is. I reckon he'll just slink back to the hills now and stay there."

Tessa could only hope so. She certainly couldn't imagine Hod riding his mule to Tulsa to hunt for her. In fact, she couldn't imagine Hod in Tulsa at all.

As the yellow taxi traveled the miles from the Glenn Pool, it came to Tessa that there was no more tearing and pulling inside of her. She felt strangely at peace.

By the time they crossed the Arkansas River bridge, she felt bone weary and thought longingly of her own bed. A soft rosy sunset still lingered over the river turning the ripply water a pale peach color.

"Wish I could drop you at your doorstep," Lendy said, "but Pole say to leave you where I gets you this morning."

"You've done more than enough," Tessa told him. "It's a short walk from here." He figured out the fare and stated the figure. Tessa added a little more and handed it over to him as he pulled up near the trolley stop. He doffed his hat as he pocketed the coins. "It's been a purety pleasure, Miss Jurgen. Pole and Chloe and the laundry women at the Patton's all speaks mighty highly of you."

As the cab drove off, Tessa breathed in deeply of the sweet spring air. Somewhere nearby there was honeysuckle in bloom. As she turned to cross Elgin, around the corner, out of nowhere, came the red roadster with a grim Gaven at the wheel.

Chapter 16

He pulled up beside her and reached over to open the door on the passenger side. "Please get in. I think we need to talk."

Tessa didn't like his tone, nor the somber expression. Undoubtedly, he'd seen her in Lendy's cab. If he was angry, he had no right to be. She paused a moment wondering what she should do.

"Unless of course," he said coolly, "you prefer a colored man's taxi cab to my car."

The words hit like a blow to her midsection. How could he say such a thing? She kept her peace and got in. As he drove slowly out of town to Standpipe Hill, the silence in the car hung like a heavy curtain between them. Even after the motor was cut off, he sat there and stared for a time without talking. At length he said, "I wanted to take you to the Glenn Pool, Tessa. Why did you choose to go in a colored man's taxi? Can you just tell me why?" He turned to her with sad, pleading eyes. "I thought you trusted me."

"I do trust you, Gaven."

"In what way? You trust me enough to be alone with me. You trust me to drive you to church, to take you to dinner. But that's only a small measure. You don't trust me enough to let me be a part of your life. And yet you trusted a colored man—of all people." His voice broke off like a sob.

"Parts of my life are so ugly," she told him, her voice barely above a whisper. "I'm ashamed..."

"Tessa." He reached for her hand. "I want to be a part of who you are, I don't care what all that involves. Please don't shut me out. No matter what it is, it will never change how I feel about you."

She looked at the clear trusting eyes, trying to remember why she hadn't wanted him to know. Why had she thought he wouldn't understand? "My father didn't just die, Gaven. He was shot in a drunken brawl." She waited for his reaction but there was none. His dark eyes were steady, unflinching.

"Moonshine whiskey kept him in a constant turmoil ever since prohibition. Some before that, but much more afterward." From there she went on to explain about that effect on her quiet, loving Mama and two innocent sisters. She told how they were now safe with Pastor and Edith. Last of all, she reluctantly told him about Hod Latham and the deal for her marriage to him.

When she finished, he simply gathered her gently into his arms and held her.

"You poor darling." He patted her and rocked her as though she were a little child. The soothing effect went to the deepest place inside her where the wounds were raw and bleeding. She had needed his understanding, even though she hadn't realized it, and he gave to her freely.

"Don't be afraid to share with me," he whispered into her hair. "I want to be here for you."

It was dark when he drove her home. As they pulled up at the gate, he turned off the motor and said, "Please Tessa, no more rides with colored men. You have no idea how strong the Klan is in this city. And they're ruthless."

"But Chloe said..."

He gently touched her lips with his finger to hush her. "It was a great danger to that taxi driver as well. If someone had a mind to, they could accuse him of accosting you, and nothing you could say would ever change that accusation."

His remark sobered her. It never occurred to her that she had placed Lendy in danger not only with Hod Latham, but also with the

Klan. She could never forgive herself if she caused harm to come to him.

"Please try to back off on your overly-friendly attitude toward the blacks. I know you mean nothing by it, but it's too risky. People in the Klan don't play games, Tessa, they play for keeps. They think nothing of whippings and lynchings."

Tessa promised she'd be careful, but she still didn't feel she'd been "overly friendly." It seemed an unfair statement. As they walked arm in arm to her door she asked, "How did you happen to be at the trolley stop this evening?"

He stopped and took hold of her shoulders. "I received a call at the school. Someone saw you get in that cab this morning. The caller didn't leave a name, but it was the voice of a young girl."

"Sadella Patton."

"That was my first guess."

"She's angry with me because of Shelby, and she's trying to pay me back."

Gaven wrapped her in his arms and kissed her warmly. "What she meant for harm has worked out for our good," he whispered between kisses. "Finally, at last, you've begun to open your heart to me. Someday we'll drive down to the Glenn Pool together and I'll meet your mama and sisters, and even the pastor."

Tessa liked that idea.

LATER THAT WEEK, A letter arrived in the mail from Pastor Stedman. In it, he explained to Tessa that he'd heard from a reliable source that a bootlegging buddy of Hod Latham's had been chosen as the local Kleagle of the Klavern in that area.

"This association could pull Hod into the Klan," the letter read, "if he's not already a part. The Klan seems made-to-order for people like Hod, because it is swathed in secrecy and fed by hate and narrow-mindedness."

Tessa shivered as she remembered Hod's hate-filled eyes.

"My thought is," the letter continued, "if Hod moves with these kinds people, he may be involved in district meetings which could bring him to Tulsa. I will be praying for your continued safety. Please be extremely careful."

Tessa didn't know what to do to be extremely careful. She said a prayer and put the letter away. It was too frightening to even think about.

AS THE DAYS OF APRIL grew longer and warmer, the formal gardens around the Patton mansion bustled with activity. Black workers moved, leveled, and graded the dirt. New plantings were added, a fish pond was being built, and precise terraces were being formed on the hillside. One Friday afternoon as she and the children were leaving to take a walk, they decided to stroll out to the gardens to observe the project. There were already masses of flowering shrubs and ornamental trees about, now it appeared there would be more flowers than ever.

They watched for a time until Wesley became restless. As usual, he had marbles on his mind. "Come on, Miss Jurgen," he insisted. "You'll make me miss out on the first game." He was already skipping halfway back to the house.

As Tessa turned to go, someone shouted, "Look out!" A muscular black man pushing a wheelbarrow loaded with dirt, narrowly missed hitting her. Jumping back, her ankle gave out and she landed in a heap on the ground.

"I is so sorry," the man said. He quickly set down his load and came to see about her. Jasper was right behind him.

"Miss Tessa," Jasper said, "are you hurt?"

"Great landing, Miss Jurgen," Wesley called out, trying to contain his laughter.

She let Jasper give her a hand up. "I'm not hurt. And thanks for the compliment, Wesley."

"Whew," Jasper said, "that was close. I saw him coming right at you, and I knew you didn't see him. If he'd hit you with that wheelbarrow, you'd been mincemeat."

Tessa looked at the large full wheelbarrow, then at the black man. Now she saw that in spite of his giant size, he wasn't much older than Jasper. "I'm afraid you're right," she agreed.

"Miss Tessa, this is my friend William, but we calls him Strapper. We go to Booker T. High together."

Tessa started to shake hands, but saw that it would make the young man uncomfortable. So she simply smiled and nodded. "Pleased to meet you."

Strapper had shoulders and arms like a lumberjack. "Likewise, ma'am," he said. "Praise be to the good Lord, you ain't hurt. Bye now." With minimal effort, he picked up the handles of the heavy wheelbarrow and went straight back to work. "You sure you all right?" Jasper wanted to know. "Mama can fix ice for that ankle."

"Doesn't hurt a bit, but thanks anyway." She brushed the grass off her dress, and tried to maintain her dignity. "Say, Jasper," she asked, "how much longer till graduation day?"

"It be June first, Miss Tessa." His eyes fairly sparkled. "Hey, maybe you'd like to see an invitation."

"I'd like that very much."

"They just been ordered. I'll sees to it you get one."

"Thanks," she called back as she followed Wesley and Lucie back across the yard.

As they came around the back of the house there was Sadella sitting on the hood of her coupe. It was obvious she'd seen everything.

As they passed, she clucked her tongue. "Mmm mmm. You sure do know how to pick your black men, little Miss Tessa."

"You shut your mouth," Wesley lashed out at her. "Miss Jurgen almost got hurt. She didn't do anything wrong."

Sadella gave a cold laugh. "She just knows how to fall in the right place at the right time. Pretty cute if you ask me."

"Well, nobody asked you," Wesley said.

"Yeah, be quiet Sadie," Lucie echoed. "We like Miss Jurgen."

"Hush, children," Tessa told them, and hurried them past their sister as quickly as possible. As they continued to the school grounds, Tessa remembered what Chloe had said a few months ago about Sadella's potential for trouble. Having felt the venom, Tessa was in full agreement.

As if being run over by a wheelbarrow, and slandered by Sadella were not enough for one day, Wesley got in a fight with Andrew. Actually Tessa wasn't surprised. The two of them had been at odds for quite some time. Andrew obviously didn't like Wesley invading his territory.

As usual, Tessa and Lucie sat beneath the cottonwood which was now fully leafed out, providing more than imaginary shade. They liked to look for four leaf clovers and braid dandelion chains while Wesley played with the boys on the school grounds. Sometimes Gaven would stop and chat, but usually he worked in his classroom after school.

Lucie saw them first. "Uh oh," she said. "Something's wrong." She pointed to where Gaven was walking across the vacant lot with his arm around Wesley's shoulder. Wesley's shirt was torn and dirty, his eye blackened, and his lip bleeding.

"Andrew started it," Wesley said before they even reached the spot where Tessa was sitting.

"I washed him up the best I could," Gaven told her almost apologetically. "And he's right, Andrew did start it."

"I don't think that's going to make any difference to his parents." Tessa stood and began folding the blanket and flung it over her arm. "I wish you could have avoided it, Wesley."

He nodded. "Me too. I tried. I really did."

"I believe you. Come on, we'd better get home." She looked over at Gaven. "Thanks for looking after him. I probably shouldn't have let him go off alone."

"The principal says if he's going to be fighting with our school children, he'll not be welcome back on the playground, even if it is after school."

She nodded. "That's understandable." She looked at Wesley. The eye was coloring fast. She would ask Chloe what to do about it. "What was the fight about? Marbles?"

Wesley shook his head.

"What then?"

He squinted up at her. "First, he said I was a baby because I had a nanny, then he said my nanny was a nigger lover."

There were those dreadful word again. As though it were a crime to love.

"I guess Andrew has put a few facts together," Gaven said to Tessa. She knew he was referring to the night of the New Year's party. That was a long time ago. She nodded. So, Wesley had defended her honor. It made her feel sad and glad all at the same time.

"Come on, pal." She put her arm around Wesley's shoulder. "Let's get home."

The Pattons were furious. Nothing she could say made any difference. Mrs. Patton especially was livid that Tessa let Wesley out of her sight for even a moment. "Henry," she said to her husband as Tessa sat in his office, "I told you we never should have hired this mere child."

To Tessa she said through tight lips, "This is to let you know, Miss Jurgen, that you are now on probation. Should one other incident like this occur, I can assure you, we will let you go that very day."

"Yes ma'am." She wanted to point out the fact that Wesley was studying more and making higher grades than before she arrived, but that didn't seem to matter. Losing the position wasn't a point of fear for Tessa. However, she now felt such a kinship with Wesley and Lucie, it would be difficult to have to leave them.

Once she was dismissed, she rose to go. "Just one more thing," Mrs. Patton said, almost as an afterthought. "Word has come to us that y'all are quite chummy with the nigras we have here. This looks bad for us, and is a ghastly example for the children. We speak to our nigras only when necessary and even then, only as it pertains to the business of the household. While you are in our employ we'll ask that you do the same."

Tessa wanted to lash out in her own defense. How could they ask her to give up her friendly talks with Chloe in the kitchen? Chloe had become a bright light in her life, and Tessa wasn't planning to let go that easily. Without answering she walked out and closed the office door behind her.

Chapter 17

The old settlers and the Indians in and around Tulsa were predicting a scorcher summer. Tessa agreed with them when the first week of May was already warm enough to be very uncomfortable as she and the children conducted lessons each day.

"We're so hot, we can't think about words and numbers," Lucie complained one morning.

Both the children had been cranky and irritable, getting on one another's nerves and having little spats. Kipsee lay panting in a cool corner. The windows were thrown wide open, but there wasn't a breath of air. Two humming electric fans kept a bit of air moving about the room. Even a lemonade break in the afternoon failed to help, so Tessa simply allowed them to play quietly even though they hadn't earned the playtime.

The evening brought little coolness as Tessa walked to the Literary Guild meeting at the church. She sometimes took the trolley part of the way, but walking allowed her the quiet time to think. And tonight she was going over the reading she was to present at the meeting. She would be reciting "Lilacs" by Amy Lowell. She loved the way the poet described the month of May.

May is a white cloud behind pine-trees
Puffed out and marching upon a blue sky.
May is a green as no other,
May is much sun through small leaves...

"Much sun" certainly described May in Tulsa. The ladies appreciated the coolness of the church basement for their meeting.

Several commented on the stillness in the air. They said it meant a big storm was brewing. Tessa knew how fast a thunderstorm could explode on the scene in Oklahoma and wished she'd brought along an umbrella. But her mind had been on her presentation.

By the time the meeting was over and the ladies came out onto the steps of the church, lightning was cutting jagged streaks in the west. She and Pauline walked a few blocks together before parting company at Denver Street. As they said their good-byes, the first cool wind whipped around them.

"It's coming a bad one," Pauline said. "You'd best get a move on. And thanks again for the wonderful reading. You're far and above the best reader we've ever had."

"I'm not sure I believe you," Tessa called out as she hurried on. "But I appreciate the compliment anyway."

Before she was halfway home, the wind was whipping in crazy directions, and the rain had started to fall. Tree limbs bent and swayed in the wind. She heard one snap. She'd surely be drenched before she reached home. Hopefully there were no twisters in the area.

The blare of a horn sounded from the street as an old farm truck rumbled up. Through the rain, she saw the window being rolled down. Terror gripped her as she saw the hooded eyes of Hod Latham. Pastor Stedman had been right.

"There you is, little lady!" he called out through the wail of the wind and the crash of the thunder. "Me and my friend, Ralph, been searching all over this blasted city for you." The door to the old truck slowly creaked opened. "You know what month this is, Tessa Jurgen? This here is May. And this here's the month you're to be my woman. I come to collect the debt owed me."

Her mind raced. She knew no one on this street. She screamed as his square hulk came across the street toward her. The screams were drowned out by the wind. She broke to run, but she was no match for him. As he grabbed for her, she tripped and fell. Cold water from the puddles soaked through to her skin. Hod stood there staring down at her. A skinny older man was now by his side.

"She sure is purty, Hod. You got you a good one."

"Thank ya, Ralph. But she's feisty." As Hod reached down for her, she kicked at his hand with all her might and he hollered in pain. "Dadburn it, woman. You dern near kicked my finger clean off." As he grabbed at his finger, she jumped up to run again. But he grabbed her arm before she could get far. Now she was kicking, screaming and trying to bite. Pain shot through her shoulder as he twisted her arm. She knew if he got her into that truck, no one would ever find her.

Suddenly, out of nowhere Strapper and Jasper were there. "Let her go," Strapper ordered.

Hod stopped and stared at the pair. "I don't take orders from no niggers."

Strapper came closer, towering over Hod's square frame. Jasper was by his side. "Let the lady go," Strapper repeated. He grabbed one of Hod's arms, and Jasper grabbed the other, and she was free. The other man was already running back to the truck. Hod cried out in pain as Strapper twisted his arm and marched him across the street and shoved him into the truck. "You needs to go back where you come from," Tessa heard him say.

"Follow me," Jasper said to Tessa. "I'll take you home the back way, so he can't follow."

As she followed Jasper down a back alley, above the sound of the wind, she heard Hod shouting, "Just wait till the Klan hears about you nigger boys attacking law-abiding citizens!"

In a matter of minutes Jasper had her at the mansion. "Let's get you to the kitchen. Mama's still there."

She followed him, unable to answer. She was shivering from the cold rain, and unable to catch her breath. Pain coursed through her side and deep into her lungs.

Chloe's face registered shock as the two entered the kitchen. "Land sakes girl. Get yourself in here. Let's get you warmed up."

Within minutes Chloe had her wrapped in a dry blanket and fixed a cup of hot lemon-honey toddy for her to sip. But the shivering wouldn't stop. Even after she was warm, the icy fingers of fear clutched at her. Jasper stood quietly by the door and waited. She tried to explain to Chloe what had happened and how Strapper and Jasper forced Hod to let her go. Her breath was short and it was hard to talk. Hard to think.

"I don't know what would have happened if they hadn't..."

"Now you hush, child. No needs to think what if. The Good Lord ain't gonna let no mean old man tote you away. He watching over you all the time."

Finally, Tessa insisted that she go on to her room and go to bed.

"You don't have to go yet, child," Chloe said patting her, comforting her. "A few minutes before you and Jasper come in the door, that little red roadster pulled up to the gate. Suppose your beau was out looking for you in this storm?"

Tessa took another long swallow of the strong hot toddy. If it had been Gaven who confronted Hod rather than Strapper, Hod might have hurt him. Or worse, Hod might have killed him. She couldn't bear to think of it.

"Maybe I could call the boarding house," she said jumping up. "I have the number."

"I'll check the library," Jasper said, "to see if it's empty." He left and returned with Pole.

"Course you can use the library phone," Pole told her. "Nobody in there now."

"I'll just be a minute," she told them. On shaky legs she made her way to the library and called. The person who answered had Gaven on the line quickly.

"Tessa! Thank God you're all right. That was a wicked storm. I hear a twister set down north of town. I was so worried about you."

"I'm fine now, Gaven."

"Why did you start out in the storm? Why didn't you call me to come and get you? Or ask for a ride from one of the ladies?"

"It came so fast." She felt like a disobedient child the way he was talking to her. "There was no storm when I left the church."

"Surely you could tell from the hot, still air. That always means a bad storm."

"Gaven, Hod found me. He tried to get me in a truck with him."

There was silence, then a mumbled, "Dear God." Then he was quiet again.

"Gaven?"

"How did you get away?"

"Jasper and a friend of his came along."

"Black boys?"

"His friend is a giant and he wasn't a bit afraid..."

"Tessa, why didn't you call me? I would have taken you safely home." His voice had an edge to the tone. "You wouldn't have needed black boys."

Tessa felt her insides wrenching. What was he saying? She drew a deep breath. "Well I didn't call you. In fact, it never even crossed my mind. And I needed the boys, and the Lord sent them along at the just the right moment. If it offends you, I'm sorry. That's just the way it is."

"Shall I come over?"

"Don't bother. I'm cold, wet, and tired. I'm going to bed." She thought he started to say something else, but she hung up.

Tessa lay awake into the late-night hours. Gaven hadn't even seemed relieved that she hadn't been carried away by Hod. Only that she'd been rescued by blacks. How could his thinking be so twisted? She tossed and turned and wondered. She'd thought at times that perhaps he was the one she'd want to belong to for the rest of her life.

But now she wasn't so sure. How could she be joined to one who had so little regard for others? Perhaps it would be best if she returned the pearls and stopped seeing him.

When her thoughts moved away from Gaven, they seemed to move back to Hod and his harsh laugh, his deep-set cold eyes, and his rancid odor. She couldn't shake the awful feeling of his grabbing at her.

TO HER GREAT DISMAY, Gaven agreed that they should stop seeing one another for a time. But he adamantly refused to take back the pearls. "I want you to have them, Tessa. They belong to you."

They had taken a short drive the evening after the storm to talk. But conversing was stiff and unnatural. Obviously he felt justified in his anger, and she could see no reason at all for his anger.

"We treat the blacks well in Tulsa," he said to her in a matter-of-fact tone. "I know you don't see it or understand it, but they're better off here than in many other cities. They're happy here."

"As long as they stay in their own place?"

"If that's how you want to put it. But it's better that way. If you'd grown up around them, then you might understand."

"Then I'm glad I grew up with my loving Mama teaching me that God loves all His children—not just a few."

"I didn't say God doesn't love the blacks."

"Then if *He* loves them, what's wrong with me loving them?"

Gaven heaved a sigh. "Tessa, you're impossible. It's a cultural thing here. It's just the way things are. And as much as I hate Klan activities—it's still a very real threat."

As he walked her back to her apartment, he simply said, "We just need time apart to think this all out."

That night she cried herself to sleep.

MAY GREW HOTTER. TESSA worked hard to finish up the children's studies. She'd been told that during June she would be going with the family on a trip. Perhaps to the seashore. It would be a relief to get away. It hurt deeply to see Gaven at church and not to be a part of his life.

On a Friday evening, the last week in May, she was sitting alone in her apartment when she heard knocking on the downstairs door. She looked down from the open window. It was Chloe.

"Chloe? What is it?"

"Oh hurry, please, child." Panic sounded in her voice. "I gots to talk to you."

Tessa ran down the steps to let Chloe in. Never, since her first night there, had Chloe ever been in her apartment. Now she was sobbing uncontrollably. "It's Jasper. They gots him."

"Who, Chloe? Who has him?" She helped her friend up the steps.

"In jail. Him and Strapper both. They in jail."

"Jail? Why? What did they do?" She got Chloe to a chair and got her a clean handkerchief.

She spoke in short spurts. "Jasper call me. Police come after them at the school and takes them away. Says they accosted a girl."

"What girl? Where?"

"Oh, Miss Tessa." She looked up through tear-filled eyes. "It be Sadella Patton."

Tessa felt the breath go out of her. "No! Surely she wouldn't. She wouldn't be that cruel."

"She done it already. Jasper say she was with the police to identify them."

Tessa struggled to get her wits about her. Why would Sadella do such a thing? What reason? "Chloe, I'll go talk to Mr. and Mrs. Patton.

They'll put a stop to this. And my cousin, Erik, works at the paper. I'll talk to him too. We'll get to the bottom of this."

Chloe pressed the handkerchief to her mouth to try to stifle her convulsive sobs. Tessa reached over to hold her and to comfort her as much as possible.

She made an appointment for Saturday morning to see the Pattons, but they were deaf to her pleading. "Are you saying our daughter is a liar?" Mrs. Patton asked. "She says those boys came at her in an alley downtown when she was simply walking from the courthouse to her car."

Mr. Patton wasn't as vocal, but sat stone-faced tapping his fingers on his desk as his wife talked.

"And what did she say Jasper did when he came *at her*?" Tessa asked.

"Isn't that enough? If two black boys came at me in an alley, I certainly wouldn't stay around to see what they had in mind."

"And what was she doing in the alley?" Tessa wanted to know.

"Taking a short cut, she told us. That's of no matter, she has a witness—a man by the name of Latham."

"Hod Latham?"

"That's the man."

"Mrs. Patton, Hod Latham is a whiskey runner with the scruples of a polecat. His word is worth nothing."

"At any price, it's worth more than that of a black man. And besides, what interest do you have in this messy incident anyway?" Mrs. Patton asked. "I believe you've been instructed to keep yourself apart from the nigras who work here."

Tessa could see she was getting nowhere, and asked to be excused. It was now quite clear, the only place a girl like Sadella would ever meet a man like Hod Latham would be at a Klan meeting. A perfect place for Sadella to feed her appetite for hate, and her desperate need for acceptance. What a tragedy.

Tessa's next stop was the newspaper office. She'd already seen the first headlines which were more frightening than she could have imagined. The *World* and *Tribune* both were calling for "justice." But she knew what that meant. The vigilante kind of justice which excluded judge and jury.

As she came flying into the newspaper office with the morning newspaper in her hand, she saw Erik across the room through the haze of blue smoke. For a moment she was taken off guard by all the eyes on her. The clacking of typewriter keys fell silent.

"Tessa, what on earth are you doing here?" He came toward her as he spoke.

She waved the newspaper at him. "How can you stand to be a part of this, Erik? These two boys did nothing wrong."

"Tessa please." Erik glanced nervously about and shoved her back out the door. "Pull yourself together. Let's go down to the coffee shop. We can talk there." He had a firm grip on her arm, steering her down the hall toward the elevator.

"Erik, I know these boys. They wouldn't hurt anyone."

"Keep your voice down, Tessa."

"Why should I keep my voice down when I'm right? I don't understand."

"You want me to lose my job?" His words were a hoarse whisper.

"What good's a job where you wind up hurting innocent people?"

She held her peace until the elevator operator opened at the ground floor. Erik led her to a corner table in the coffee shop and ordered each of them a cup of black coffee. She didn't even like coffee.

"Tessa, you've got to calm down and stay out of this."

"But Jasper saved my life, Erik. He and his friend Strapper. If they hadn't come along, I don't know where I'd be right now. Maybe dead. Don't you understand?"

Erik shook his head. "Don't Tessa. Don't let this get to you. You've got to detach yourself. You don't understand the power of the Klan here. Tessa, they not only lynch, they tar and feather and brand with acid. They're ruthless."

"How can you be afraid of the Klan? You were in the war. Surely you faced worse than this."

"Maybe that's the problem," he said, shaking his blond head, "I've seen enough fighting and killing to last me a long, long time."

"These boys need someone on their side."

"And you think it has to be you? Let me tell you something, Tessa. You keep on trying to speak up for black folk here in Tulsa, and the Klan will gladly see you lynched right alongside those black boys. Let all the blacks in Greenwood be on their side—not you. I hear they're gathering arms and ammunition right now."

Tessa jumped to her feet. "Erik Torsten, let me tell you something, I'd rather hang with them than be a coward and desert them."

She heard him calling after her, but she didn't look back.

Chapter 18

Tessa returned to the mansion in a daze. She was shocked that there was no one in the city to speak up in the defense of Jasper and his friend. No one.

She could hear the sounds of Chloe's weeping before she reached the kitchen door. Gently, quietly, she pushed open the door and saw Chloe sitting at the table holding a Bible to her bosom, weeping and rocking back and forth. "My baby. My Jasper. Oh Lord, my poor baby."

She knew what Chloe feared, and there was nothing Tessa could do to quiet those fears. She walked over to the table and pulled up another chair beside her, putting her arms around the trembling shoulders.

"They wouldn't listen to you, would they?" she said. "Ain't nobody gonna listen to a black boy. My Jasper wouldn't hurt nobody."

Tessa held her and said nothing.

"Preacher Sam says I oughtn't to try to go see Jasper. Says it could cause a worse ruckus." She looked up at Tessa with tear-filled eyes. "Now tell me how there could be worse ruckus than this? He say they might not even let me in, beings I'm black."

"I'll go, Chloe."

Chloe pulled a kerchief from her apron pocket and wiped her nose. "To see him? To see my Jasper?"

Tessa nodded. "What do you want me to take?"

Chloe seemed to calm a bit. She held out the book. "This here's Jasper's Bible. See how worn it is? That boy love God's word. He always reading his Bible. He be lost without it." She smoothed the black leather cover in loving strokes. "I give it to him when he was knee-high to a grasshopper. He wanted his own so bad. Wouldn't shush begging, till he had his very own."

"What else shall I take? Got some cookies? Cake? Both boys would love that."

"Mmm, mmm. You right about that, child." She seemed to come to life again. "Let me get a basket and we'll put a few things in. You being white, they'll let you take more stuff in."

Black, white; white, black. Tessa was sick to death of the words. Why should it matter so much?

Chloe got a basket from a high shelf, then shook her head. "I must be getting addled. You can't go now. It'd be evening before you gets back. No sense you courting more trouble being out after dark. Especially with all that's going on right now. You go tomorrow."

"After church, Chloe. I'll go right after church."

Chloe left the basket on the cabinet and came to where Tessa was standing. "I'm beholding to you for wanting to help."

Tessa gave her a hug and left.

WHEN TESSA CAME HOME from church the next morning, there was a note tacked to her door that the Pattons wanted to see her. Excitement rose inside her. Perhaps Sadella has confessed that she'd made up the entire story. Perhaps now the boys would be freed.

Her tap at Mr. Patton's office door was answered by a gruff, "Come in." Mr. Patton was alone. He did not offer her a chair. His stiff starched white collar was snugged up under the roundness of his chin. His shiny hair was slicked back; his mouth was set tight. He looked straight at her. "Miss Jurgen, word has come to me that you have plans to go to the jail this afternoon to visit those boys who accosted my daughter. Is that right?"

The walls in this house must have ears. How could he have known so quickly? "Sundays are my day off," she said, forcing her voice not to waver. "Since when have you asked me what I'm doing on my own time?"

"I'll not have an employee of mine making me look bad in this community. I don't need more scandal. I'm telling you to stay away from that jail."

"Mr. Patton, I don't believe for a moment that you've been taken in by your daughter's story. Those boys are innocent. They're scared and they're lonely. There's no telling what's going to happen to them. Chloe wants Jasper to have his Bible. Are you going to tell me this boy shouldn't have his own Bible?"

"Sure he can have his Bible." He slowly rolled his leather chair up to the desk and straightened in the chair. Pointing at her, he said, "But you'd better not be the one who delivers it. That's all." He waved her away with his hand.

Tessa didn't tell Chloe about the conversation. She merely took the basket and went on her way. She was surprised to find a small crowd gathered around the courthouse downtown. *Oh God*, she prayed, *don't let a mob be forming already.*

The sun was hot and the air still. Her broad-brimmed straw hat shaded her eyes from the glaring sun. Sweat trickled down her back and her cotton dress clung to her body. When the light turned green she walked across the intersection toward the courthouse. Someone yelled, "Look there, she's taking a basket up to those black boys."

It was Sadella sitting on the hood of her coupe, surrounded by a group of her young friends. Probably a few who were at her party the night Tessa helped Jasper get away. There were other hoots and catcalls as she proceeded closer to the crowd. Cars were parked helter-skelter around the courthouse.

Suddenly there was a tug on her arm. She turned to look into the troubled eyes of Gaven MacIntyre. "Tessa, what on earth are you doing? Trying to start a riot?"

"Of course not. I'm trying to help a friend."

"Erik told me you might try something like this, but I didn't believe him. Tessa, don't do this."

Tessa pulled her arm loose from his grasp. "I'm taking this boy his Bible and a few things to eat. What could be so wrong?"

His voice was strained with emotion. "Don't you see this crowd? They're just looking for something to get riled up about."

"Then why don't the police send them all home?"

Gaven shook his head. "Tessa, you're not listening."

Tessa stopped a moment and looked at Gaven's soft eyes, and the fine lines of his square-set chin. She remembered his embrace and his gentle words of love to her. If he loved her, why couldn't he understand? Now she reached out for *his* arm. "Gaven, these two boys risked their lives for me. And Jasper's mother is my dear friend. How could I live with myself if I deserted them now? I can't do much, but I can do this."

She turned and proceeded toward the front door of the court house and walked slowly up the steps. The hoots and hollers were louder now. Inside the cool building, her heels clicked on the marble floor. She took the elevator to the top floor where the jail was located.

The guard riffled through Jasper's Bible until Tessa feared the pages would be torn clean out. Then he broke open each cookie and poked his pocket knife all through the layered chocolate cake. "Okay lady, you can go on in. But why you want to visit a couple of niggers, is beyond me."

He unlocked the cell to give them the food, then allowed Tessa to stand outside the cell to visit. The boys were relieved to see her. They thanked her repeatedly for coming, and especially for bringing the Bible. When they asked her what was happening outside, she couldn't tell them, for she really didn't know.

"It seems like a harmless crowd of curious onlookers," she said. "Some are young people."

"What do you think they're waiting to see?" Strapper asked. She shook her head, terrified to even think of the answer.

"We didn't do nothing," Jasper said solemnly. "I swear. We was nowhere near Miss Sadella."

"I know that. And I suspect Mr. and Mrs. Patton believe it as well. But pride won't let them speak truth. Boys, I know who Sadella has called on as her eye witness." She grasped the coldness of the steel bars. "It's the man you saved me from the night of the storm. His name is Hod Latham. He's from the hill country near my home."

"I knowed he was bad," Strapper said, shaking his head. "I could see that the way he was trying to hurt you."

"The awful hate inside of Hod," she said, "has now mixed with the hate inside of Sadella Patton. And it's a frightful mixture."

"You shouldn't have come, Miss Tessa," Jasper said. "Now they be after you."

"I know you're in here partly because of me. I wanted you to know I'll never forget what you did for me. I'll be eternally grateful."

Strapper looked solemn. "We'd do it again in a wink."

"We done it 'cause you a fine lady, Miss Tessa," Jasper told her. "A real fine lady." He pulled out a piece of paper. "This is for my Mama. Will you see to it she gets it?"

Tessa tucked the note down inside her shoe—just in case. After barely ten minutes the guard said her time was up. She said a quick prayer with the two of them before leaving.

When she emerged from the courthouse, the crowd had grown some. Again, there were rude remarks. She held her head high and went on her way without hurrying.

When she reached Galveston, she saw a flat-bed truck rumbling down the street toward her. Chloe was on the rider side. Pole was riding on the back with two other black men she didn't know. Lendy was driving.

Chloe jumped out of the truck and ran over to her quite out of breath. "We been waiting for you, Miss Tessa. We come to take you, 'cause the Pattons done put you out."

Chapter 19

A t first Chloe's words didn't register. Tessa's mind was still on the image of two innocent boys sitting in a jail cell. "Put me out?"

Chloe reached out and gently touched her arm. "Miss Tessa, they done took all your nice things and just put them out on the driveway."

So that was it. She paid the price and the price was the loss of her job and her cozy, beautiful apartment. The shock was beginning to set in. What would she do with no job?

"Now you stays right here. No need for you to see it. It's not a pretty sight. We load it all up and come back here and get you. You come stay at my house a few days till all this stinky mess blow over."

She could only nod. Chloe's son was in jail, and still she was thinking of others. It was beyond all that Tessa could comprehend. Standing there waiting, she thought of Lucie and Wesley. The three of them were going to wind up lessons next week and celebrate with a last-day-of-school party. She had even let them make the plans. She was going to miss them.

Suddenly the hot glaring sun made her feel queasy and weak. She moved toward the coolness of a shade tree and leaned heavily against the rough trunk. As she gazed down the street she caught sight of Shelby emerging from the side door of his house. He was walking purposefully toward her. God forbid! Shelby Harland was the last person she wanted to talk to.

"Tessa!" he called out as his steps quickened. "I just heard. I can't believe the gall of those Pattons."

Word spread in this town like wildfire. Tessa stepped back as he came nearer. She didn't want him to touch her.

"Now don't you worry about a thing," he crooned, "I've talked to my parents and you're more than welcome to come and stay with us until you find a place. Or forever for that matter." He stepped nearer and she drew away. "Tessa, I just want to help. Why won't you let me help you? See that big house?" He pointed back toward their sprawling red-brick mansion. "There are rooms to spare and more. I'll have one of our men go get your things—you just say the word."

"Please just leave me alone."

"It's the best offer you've got, Tessa."

Chloe's shout from down the street interrupted them. "Miss Tessa! Come quick. Mr. Patton done want to talk to you."

"Maybe I do have a better offer, Mr. Harland." She hurried off in the direction of Chloe's voice.

"Sorry, but I had to fib a little," Chloe said when she was within hearing. "Mr. Patton don't want to talk to you. I just aim to get you away from that Harland fella. Was he offering to rescue you?"

"Exactly. How did you know?"

"I ain't sure, but I thinks Sadella and him are in cahoots."

"Cahoots? How?"

"When you is young and crazy in love, as I thinks Miss Sadella is with Mr. Shelby, you do anything he asks—even point him toward the other woman."

"But that doesn't make any sense."

"Love seldom does, Child. Now come on. You and I is taking another way to the trolley. Lendy and them done took your stuff on to my house. No sense anybody seeing you get in a truck with black folk nohow."

Chloe's house was a white frame two-story on a street lined with trim, modest houses right in the midst of Greenwood. By the time she and Chloe arrived, several of the men were busy boxing up Tessa's belongings. The lovely green coat with the silky black lining was not among them. She had diligently made payments on the coat with each and every payday. Evidently Trevalene Patton didn't think it had been enough. The remorse that shot through her, let her know how much she'd come to love that expensive coat. Other than her pearls, it was the nicest thing she'd ever owned.

By nightfall, her personal items were neatly placed in an upstairs bedroom, and her other things, carefully boxed up, were moved to the basement.

Tessa was so utterly exhausted she nearly forgot Jasper's letter until she kicked off her shoes in her room. She jumped back into her shoes and hurried downstairs. Chloe's husband, Willard, had just arrived home. Tessa could see Jasper's features in his father. The older man was tall and slender, but with bulging neck and shoulder muscles. His eyes were full of despair, as were Chloe's. He shook her hand when Chloe introduced them, and thanked her warmly for all she'd done for Jasper.

"Your son is a bright, talented young man," Tessa told him. "I only wish I could do more for him."

He shook his head and gave a slight smile. "You done plenty."

She didn't stay while the parents read the letter from their incarcerated son, but wasted no time getting ready for bed. She wanted to lie there and consider her predicament. Tomorrow she would call Pastor Stedman and ask for his advice. Maybe it was time to get back to the Glenn Pool. She barely finished the thoughts before falling into a sound sleep.

Suddenly she bolted upright at the sound of the most pitiful cry of anguish she'd ever heard. For a moment, she was unable to remember where she was. It was dark except for the soft glow of street lights outside the window. Another cry sounded ending in a wailing sob.

Without thinking, she pulled on her robe and slippers and went flying down the stairs. A number of black people were gathered in Chloe's front room Chloe was seated on the davenport wrapped in the ample arms of a large black woman.

"Oh my God, no. Please no. Not my baby!" The sobbing cries were coming from Chloe as the large woman rocked her as though she were a small child.

One of the men looked up to see Tessa coming down the stairs, and nudged Willard. Then Chloe saw her. "Oh Miss Tessa, Miss Tessa, they killed him. They killed my baby. My baby."

The words seemed faint and far away. As Tessa felt her knees go weak, she grabbed for the banister. An older heavyset man came to her. "You must be Miss Jurgen. Come out to the kitchen with me please." He assisted her down the hall to the kitchen in the back of the house. After Tessa was seated at the table, he said. "They call me Preacher Sam, and that's my wife, Mama Sue, in there with Chloe."

Another black lady who was already in the kitchen set a steaming cup of hot tea before her. "What happened?" Tessa asked although in her heart she didn't want to know.

"A mob gathered and took the boys out around midnight. The jailer didn't even put up no fuss. Just opened up and let 'em be taken away." He seated his large frame in a chair next to her, and the chair creaked in protest. "They lynched Jasper, but somehow Strapper got away. We think they didn't try hard to find him, figuring they can sic the bloodhounds on him come daylight."

They hung a boy—a mere boy. It wasn't possible. A convulsion grabbed at her midsection and she wondered for a moment if she were going to be sick. She tried to steady her hand to sip the strong tea.

"We sent men out to find Strapper—to get him out of the state if possible."

A fresh wave of crying and sobbing sounded from the front room. Tessa was sure it was going to tear her heart out.

"Chloe tells us that you gots a cousin what works at the World newspaper," the preacher was saying.

"Yes I do," she managed to answer. "His name is Erik Tornsten.

"You think you could get him to come here and listen to us? Could we talk to him?"

She shook her head. "I'm not sure. I tried to talk to him just the other day about Jasper, and he turned a deaf ear. I think he loves his job too much."

"Would you try? The men of Greenwood is at the end of theyselves. They is fighting mad about this injustice. I'm feelin' something terrible is going to happen."

"Of course, I'll try. I'll do anything I can."

Then suddenly, without bidding, her own tears and sobs broke forth like an explosion which she couldn't stop. The kind woman moved from the stove to put her arms around Tessa and held her as the deep sobs shook her to her very core.

THE NEXT DAY, YET ANOTHER young black man was arrested. A bootblack boy named Dick. This time for allegedly attacking an elevator operator in the Drexel building. And now what Preacher Sam had feared, came to pass. The men of Greenwood were taking up arms. Many of the war veterans still possessed their firearms. They cleaned them, oiled them, loaded them and stood ready.

Tuesday's headlines in the *Tulsa Tribune*, were highly inflammatory and all the community feared there would be yet another lynching. The blacks determined it would not happen. It was too late now for Tessa, or anyone else, to do anything to help.

This time, the mob of whites outside the courthouse was even bigger. Word came back to Chloe's house by Tuesday evening that more than a thousand whites were crowded around the courthouse.

Tessa listened as a group of black men gathered in Chloe's front room trying to decide what to do. They'd been down to the courthouse earlier to try to help the police maintain order. They demanded that the boy, named Dick, be freed; that no more lynchings take place—but they were ordered back home. Now they felt they had no choice. They would go to back to the courthouse fully armed, and stand their ground.

Chloe and the women begged them not to go. Willard and Chloe still didn't know the whereabouts of their son's body nor when a funeral service might be held. And now this nightmare pandemonium was overshadowing Jasper's untimely death, barely giving them time to grieve.

Tessa sat up with the women long into the night. There were relatives of Chloe's, along with Finney and Elsie Mae who worked at the Patton's. Others were fellow church members. None of them seemed to mind that Tessa was in their midst.

The phone rang incessantly as sporadic news came that shooting had broken out near the courthouse. Sometime after midnight, word came that the whites were armed to military proportions, and that the National Guard might be called in.

"I tried to tell them," Chloe moaned as she paced back and forth in the kitchen. "Ain't no good never come from trying to fight back."

But Tessa could understand the desperation of their menfolk. Desperate enough to stand and fight. Sporadic gunfire was heard off and on throughout the night hours as the ladies stayed together to pray and to encourage one another. At about three, a car full of whites rumbled down Chloe's street shooting at anything that moved. Tessa found herself sprawled on the floor to dodge flying bullets.

By afternoon of the next day, the possibility of violence escalated. The women discussed the need to get Tessa to a safer place. Elsie Mae's grandma rented a house just down the street owned by a white man. "Granny's took the train to Mississippi to visit kinfolk for a spell," Elsie Mae said. "We can put Tessa down in Granny's cellar."

"That's a right fine plan, Elsie Mae," Chloe put in. "No white man gonna hurt his own property." She turned to Tessa. "We need to keep you safe, child."

"I won't leave you, Chloe," she said. "I'm staying with you."

"You shush your mouth. That's silly talk. Run upstairs and grab a few things you might need. I'll put a little food together for you."

Tessa had no idea what she would need. She could only think to grab her Bible and the velvet box containing her beloved pearls. She stopped momentarily to look out the window. Smoke rose in the air near Greenwood and Archer. Were the rioters settings fires? Surely not. But would a mob do anything less?

A gray pall of smoke draped the sky as they stepped out onto the front porch. The air was thick, and hot, and still. It was decided only Chloe and Elsie Mae would accompany Tessa to show the way. More gunfire could be heard as they ventured cautiously down the street. They stayed close to houses and ran the distances between.

They'd gone about two blocks when Elsie Mae cried out. "Oh my God! There come a white man. What we gonna do?"

"This way," Chloe ordered. "Go behind the houses."

But before they could follow, Tessa heard her name being frantically called out. Her heart stopped as she whirled around. It was Gaven racing wildly toward her. "Tessa, Tessa! Wait! Thank God I've finally found you."

"Stop Chloe," she said. "It's all right. It's Gaven."

Chloe stopped to look. "Land sakes, what that man doing in the middle of this mess? He gonna get hisself killed for sure."

"Oh thank God you're safe," Gaven spoke between deep gasps. "I've been searching everywhere for you."

Then he was beside her grabbing her into his arms. Holding her, squeezing her, rocking her. "I'm sorry Tessa. I'm so very very sorry. I've been such a blind fool. Can you ever forgive me for letting my stupid prejudices pervert my thinking."? He buried his face in her long hair. "I never knew, Tessa. I never understood what hate and prejudice could do until now. Until this."

"How's about if you two make up when we get you under cover," Chloe said. "Come on, Mr. MacIntyre, before some itchy trigger finger mistooks you for a rioter."

"The entire area is surrounded," Gaven told them as they ran together to the next house. He held Tessa's hand tightly clasped in his. "The mob is looting and burning everything. It's totally out of control."

"Around here to the back," Elsie Mae said, directing them to a white bungalow with masses of climbing roses smothering the white picket fence. "Granny won't mind. She love having company. Even when she don't know they is coming." Elsie Mae lifted the latch on the gate and led them to the back cellar door.

Tessa turned to Chloe. "Where will you go now?"

"The talk is we'll go to our church, Mt. Zion Baptist. We'll be safe there. Built like a fortress." She handed Tessa the parcel of food she'd prepared. "Now you two stay here till all this calms down." She looked at Gaven. "You take care of her."

"I promise, Chloe. And thank you."

Tessa stepped back out of the way as Gaven helped Chloe pull up the heavy cellar door. Without warning, a shot exploded out of nowhere, and Tessa felt hot, searing pain rip through her upper arm. She screamed and collapsed to the ground.

Gaven scooped her up in his arms and carefully, but quickly carried her down the stairs. Chloe started to follow him. "No, Chloe. You go on, just like you planned. Get yourselves to safety."

"We be back here soon's the shooting stops," Chloe promised.

The heavy door was lowered and all they could hear was the abbreviated bursts of distant gunfire. The basement was clean and dry with a sturdy concrete floor. There was an aroma of cool dampness. Filtered light came in through the high windows. Gaven carried her to a corner where he laid her down. Wooden shelves were lined with an abundance of fruit jars filled to the brim with a variety of fruits, pickles and preserves.

"We won't go hungry," Gaven quipped as he glanced around. Quickly and deftly, he tore the tail of his shirt and tied it tightly around her arm. "It's clean. The bullet went right through." She winced in pain.

"I'm going upstairs for a blanket. Be right back." He was soon back beside her fixing the blanket beneath her and at her back. There was a pillow for her head. "There's wine here," he said. "I'm going to use it on the wound." His words were soothing, but she could think of nothing but the white-hot pain searing her arm.

He uncorked the bottle and gently cleansed the wound, and soon the fire was reduced to a steady throb of pain. He talked steadily as he worked. "As soon as I heard of Jasper's death, I was sick with remorse, Tessa. I've been so wrong. You needed someone to stand by you and I deserted you. You were ten feet tall when you walked into that courthouse." He kissed her forehead and the top of her head, running his fingers through her hair. "I'll never desert you again. If you give me a chance, I'll never leave your side, ever. "

He set the bottle aside and sat beside her cradling her in his strong arms. "Please say you forgive me."

She took a breath. "Of course. Of course I forgive you, my darling." Her voice was a whisper. "You took such an awful chance coming here."

"You took a chance to help Jasper. You're such a little fighter. I'm so proud of you." He stroked her hair, and caressed her face. "I was frantic. I went right into the Patton's house looking for you. That girl, Sadella, said you'd gone to stay with Shelby."

"The invitation was given." Sadella had no doubt called Shelby the moment she knew that her parents planned to kick Tessa out. Poor Sadella probably thought she would gain his favor.

"At first he wouldn't tell me anything, but after I nearly shook his teeth loose and rattled his brains, he said the last he knew, you were with Chloe. Then I was sure you'd be here in Greenwood."

He opened the package of food and made her eat a little of the cornbread. "And in the midst of all this tragedy," he said, "I have good news to tell you. Erik was able to help the other boy escape to the Arkansas border."

Suddenly the pain in Tessa's arm meant nothing. "Strapper's safe?" She struggled to sit up. "Erik helped? I can't believe it. Oh thank God, he's safe."

"Erik said a black man named Preacher Sam called him asking for help."

"I met him at Chloe's house the night of the lynching."

"Erik told him he couldn't do anything at the paper, but he worked with two of the black men to find the boy before the posse did. A friend of Erik's in Fort Smith is hiding him till things cool over."

She leaned back into Gaven's arms. She'd been terrified of what they might do to Strapper if they found him. Now her mind was at rest. He was safe.

"Tessa, I honestly never knew my thinking about the blacks was wrong."

"I know, Gaven. I know."

"They were never people to me before. They were just... They were just *there*. They stayed where they belonged and everything was all right. Most everyone I know thinks the same way. My friends, my family—even at church."

"I know. I've felt it."

"I see differently now, Tessa. Because of you, I see people. *Real people*."

She took a breath. "That change of heart must cause your Father-God to rejoice."

The talking was draining her strength. When she finished the cornbread, Gaven insisted she take a swallow or two of the wine. "It'll help you sleep," he said.

It smelled sweet and good, but the bitter taste was terrible, burning her throat. He situated her close beside him, her head on his shoulder, her wounded arm lying across her stomach.

"What's this?" he asked, feeling at her side.

She was getting drowsy now. "The velvet box in my pocket. Chloe told me to take a few things so I grabbed my pearls and my Bible."

He drew the box from her pocket and opened it. "I want you to have them on," he insisted. "If anything happens in the night, I want you to be wearing them."

It took a great deal of effort to raise her head so he could fasten the clasp at her neck. She felt the sweetness of his kiss on her neck. Then she snuggled back against him.

"As soon as we get out of here, it will be a ring, my darling, rather than a string of pearls."

She was quiet.

"Well?"

"Mmm?"

"Will you wear my ring, Tessa? Will you marry me? I want you to be my wife."

The words were like a melody lulling her softly to sleep. They were the words she'd been waiting and longing to hear. She barely remembered grunting an audible "yes" before falling into a fitful sleep.

Chapter 20

The night was punctuated with horrifying sounds of gunfire, shouting, running feet and crackling fires burning. Whenever she aroused, Gaven was right there holding her, talking to her, and once he was reciting the ninety-first Psalm.

"'Thou shalt not be afraid for the terror by night; nor for the arrow that flieth by day...' The words were a soothing balm to her pain and her fear. "'There shall be no evil befall thee, neither shall any plague come nigh thy dwelling. For he shall give his angels charge over thee, to keep thee in all thy ways.'"

It was as though the stillness woke her before dawn. The nightmarish sounds were gone. "We're still safe, my darling," he told her as she opened her eyes. He gently kissed her. "How's the arm?"

"It was all right till I woke up." The wound throbbed like a drum pounding all the way to her temples.

"I'll change the dressing, then we'll eat before we go out. Sounds like the war is over. No telling how far we'll have to walk to get you to a doctor."

This time after wrapping it in clean cloth, he ripped the edge of the blanket to fashion a makeshift sling.

Her bones felt stiff from lying all night on a concrete floor, but she found she was able to walk. She stood nearby as Gaven strained to push open the heavy wooden cellar door. Then she heard him gasp as he looked out. "Oh dear God."

He came down to help her up the steps. Nothing could have prepared her for the vast wasteland of destruction that met her eyes. The rows upon rows of sturdy, proud homes lay in blackened cinders. For miles in all directions, only a few houses were left standing. Puffy curls of smoke drifted lazily upward. The prosperous community of Greenwood had been brought to its knees.

"It's like the war," Gaven whispered. "Only in France we knew why we were fighting. This is all so senseless."

"Hate will always destroy," she said.

As they moved out to the street, Chloe and Elsie Mae were walking toward them. The two women looked weary and haggard. "Miss Tessa, thank God you all right," Chloe called out. "We come to see."

"I'm taking her to a doctor," Gaven said.

"I hopes you find one." Chloe was next to them now. Her dress was black from soot. There were burns on her arm. Elsie Mae's face was cut and bleeding.

"Chloe what happened? Your arm..."

"Child, they done burned our church. Our big new beautiful church is in ashes." She choked back tears. "They burn most everything. All our men be taken away at gunpoint. I hear they's holding them at the fairgrounds. So much shooting and burning. They was shooting as we tried to run out of the church to get away from the fire. No telling how many dead. I don't even know if Willard is still alive."

"Come with us, Chloe," Gaven said. "We'll help you."

"Not now. I gots to help the other women with the little ones. We gots to set up some kind of shelter." She came to give Tessa one more hug. "My house was partly burned, I hear tell, but I hopes your things in the cellar be safe."

As Tessa surveyed the terrible destruction, her own belongings held little importance. She was thankful to be alive.

Chloe turned to Gaven. "You take care of this little sweetie now. You hear?"

"I will, Chloe," he said putting his arm around Tessa.

Chloe and Elsie Mae turned and walked slowly back down the street.

Chloe stopped momentarily to call back over her shoulder. "Tessa? This here woulda been Jasper's graduation day." Then she went on.

Tessa didn't even bother to wipe away the stream of tears washing down her cheeks.

Gaven held her close. "I will always wish I'd walked by your side through that crowd into the jail."

She looked up at his strong face and his tear-filled eyes and knew he meant every word. "They'll need help rebuilding," she told him.

"We'll be right here to help. Together."

Arm in arm they walked away through the smoldering rubble.

Norma Jean Lutz Bio

Norma Jean Lutz's writing career began professionally in the 1970s when she enrolled in a writing correspondence course. Since then, she has had over 250 short stories and articles published in both secular and Christian publications. The full-time writer is also the author of over 50 published books under her own name and many ghostwritten books. Her books have been favorably reviewed in *Affair de Coeur, Coffee Time Romance, Romance Reader at Heart, and The Romance Studio* magazines, and her short fiction has garnered a number of first prizes in local writing contests.

Norma Jean is the founder of the Professionalism In Writing School, which was held annually in Tulsa for fourteen years. This writers' conference, which closed its doors in 1996, gave many writers their start in the publishing world.

A gifted teacher, Norma Jean has taught a variety of writing courses at local colleges and community schools, and is a frequent speaker at writers' seminars around the country. For eight years, she taught on staff for the Institute of Children's Literature. She has served as artist-in-residence at elementary schools, and for two years taught a staff development workshop for language arts teachers in schools in Northeastern Oklahoma.

As co-host for the Tulsa KNYD Road Show, she shared the microphone with Kim Spence to present the Road Show Book Club, a feature presented by the station for more than a year. She has also appeared in numerous interviews on KDOR-TV.

As a writer who loves writing for teens, and hanging out with teens, Norma Jean has launched the **Clean Teen Reads** website and blog. Lots of fun stuff for teens! Check it out here:

www.CleanTeenReads.net[1]

The Site for Teens Who Love Books and Stories

---

1. http://www.CleanTeenReads.net

Other Titles by Norma Jean Lutz

The Tulsa Series

#1 Tulsa Tempest (Christian historical romance)
#2 Tulsa Turning (Christian historical romance)
#3 Tulsa Trespass (Christian historical romance)
#4 Return to Tulsa (Christian historical romance)

The Norma Jean Lutz Classic Collection

1. *Flower in the Hills* (a sweet teen romance)
2. *Tiger Beetle at Kendallwood* (a sweet teen romance)
3. *Rockin' into Romance* (a sweet teen romance)
4. *Oklahoma Exile* (a sweet teen romance)
5. *Forever is Over* (a pre-teen novel about friendship)
6. *Lingering Dreams* (a sweet teen romance)

Teen Coming-of-Age Action Adventure Novels

Brought To You By The Color Drab
A Noble Cause: An Honorable Man Will Uphold a Noble Cause

Don't miss out!

Visit the website below and you can sign up to receive emails whenever Norma Jean Lutz publishes a new book. There's no charge and no obligation.

https://books2read.com/r/B-A-ZJGT-VSHXC

BOOKS 2 READ

Connecting independent readers to independent writers.